Brenda Harlen is a former attorney who once had the privilege of appearing before the Supreme Court of Canada. The practice of law taught her a lot about the world and reinforced her determination to become a writer—because in fiction, she could promise a happy ending! Now she is an award-winning, RITA® Award–nominated national bestselling author of more than thirty titles for Mills & Boon. You can keep up-to-date with Brenda on Facebook and Twitter or through her website, brendaharlen.com.

Bring Me a Maverick for Christmas!

BRENDA HARLEN

MILLS & BOON

First published in Great Britain 2018
by Mills & Boon, an imprint of HarperCollins*Publishers*
1 London Bridge Street, London, SE1 9GF

Large Print edition 2019

© 2018 Harlequin Books S.A.

Special thanks and acknowledgement to Brenda Harlen
for her contribution to the Montana Mavericks:
The Lonelyhearts Ranch continuity.

ISBN: 978-0-263-08333-0

MIX
Paper from
responsible sources
FSC
www.fsc.org   FSC C007454

This book is produced from independently certified
FSC™ paper to ensure responsible forest management. For
more information visit www.harpercollins.co.uk/green.

Printed and bound in Great Britain
by CPI Group (UK) Ltd, Croydon, CR0 4YY

This book is dedicated to Ryan. I know you stopped writing letters to Santa a lot of years ago, but as you finish up your first term at university, I'm making three wishes for you this season:

1. that you eternally believe in the magic of Christmas;

2. that you always know how proud I am of you; and

3. that you forever remember how much I love you. XO

Chapter One

"No way in ho-ho-hell," Bailey Stockton said, his response to his brother's request firm and definitive.

"Hear me out," Dan urged.

"No," he said again. He'd been conscripted to help with far too much Christmas stuff already. Such as helping Luke decorate Sunshine Farm for the holidays and sampling a new Christmas cookie recipe that Eva was trying out (okay, that one hadn't been much of a hardship—the cookies, like everything she made, were delicious). His youngest brother, Jamie, had even asked him to babysit—yes, babysit!—so that he could take his wife into Kalispell to do some shopping for their triplets and enjoy a holiday show.

In fact, Bailey had been enlisted for so many tasks, he'd begun to suspect that his siblings had collectively made it their personal mission to revive his holiday spirit. Because he couldn't seem to make them understand that his holiday spirit was too far gone to be resurrected. They'd have better luck planning the burial and just letting him pretend the holidays didn't exist.

"But it's for Janie's scout troop," Dan implored.

Janie was Dan and Annie's daughter—the child his brother had only found out about when he returned to Rust Creek Falls not quite eighteen months earlier. Since then, his brother had been doing everything he could to make up for lost time. Which Bailey absolutely understood and respected; he just didn't want to be conscripted toward the effort.

"Then *you* do it," he said.

"I was planning to do it," Dan told him. "And I was looking forward to it, but I'm in bed now with some kind of bug."

"Is that a pet name for Annie?"

"Ha ha," his brother said, not sounding amused.

"Well, you don't sound very sick to me," Bailey noted.

"That's because you haven't heard me puking."

"And I don't mind missing out on that," he assured his brother.

"I need your help," Dan said again.

"I'm sorry you're not up to putting on the red suit, but there's got to be someone else who can do it."

"You don't think I tried to find someone

else?" Dan asked. "I mean, no offense, big brother, but when I think of Christmas spirit, yours is not the first name that springs to mind."

Bailey took no offense to his brother speaking the truth. But he was curious: "Who else did you ask?"

"Luke, Jamie, Dallas Traub, Russ Campbell, Anderson Dalton, even Old Gene. No one else is available. You're my last resort, Bailey, and if you don't come through—"

"Don't worry," Annie interrupted, obviously having taken the phone from her husband. "He'll come through. Won't you, Bailey?"

He hated to let them down, but what they were asking was beyond his abilities. And way outside his comfort zone. "I wish I could, but—"

That was as far as he got in formulating a response before his sister-in-law interjected again.

"You can," she said. "You just need to stop being such a Grooge."

"A *what*?"

"A Grooge," she said again. "Since you have even less Christmas spirit than either the Grinch or Scrooge, I've decided you're a Grooge."

"Definitely not Santa Claus material," he felt compelled to point out.

"Under normal circumstances, I'd agree," Annie said. "But these aren't normal circumstances and your brother needs you to step up and help out, because that's what families do. And that's why I know you're going to do this."

Chastened by his sister-in-law's brief but pointed lecture, how could he do anything else?

But he had no intention of giving in graciously. "Bah, humbug."

"I'll take that as a yes," Annie said.

Bailey could only sigh. "What time and where?"

"I'll meet you at the Grace Traub Community Center in an hour."

And so, an hour later, Bailey found himself at the community center, in one of the small activity rooms that had been repurposed as a dressing room for the event. Annie bustled around, helping him dress.

"Is this really necessary?" he asked, as she secured the padded belly.

"Of course, it's necessary. Santa's not a lean mean rancher—he's a toy maker with a milk-and-cookies belly."

He slid his arms into the big red coat and fastened the wide belt around his expanded middle.

"Now sit so that I can put on your beard and wig and fix your face," Annie said.

He sat. Then scowled. "What do you mean— fix my face?"

"Relax and let me do my thing."

"'Do my thing' are not words that inspire me to relax," he told her.

But he clenched his jaw and didn't say anything else as she unzipped a pouch and pulled out a tube that looked suspiciously like makeup. She brushed whatever it was onto his eyebrows, then took out a pot and another brush that she used on his cheeks.

"I can't believe I let you talk me into this," he grumbled.

"I know this isn't your idea of fun, but it means a lot to Dan that you stepped up."

"I didn't step," he reminded her. "I was pushed."

Her lips curved as she recapped the pot and put it back in the bag. "Now the beard," she said, and hooked the elastic over his ears.

"No one's going to thank me for this when I screw it up," he warned her.

"You're not going to screw it up."

"Beyond *ho ho ho*, I don't have a clue what to say."

"This might be a first for you, but it's not for the kids," she told him. "And if you really get stuck, I have no doubt that your wife will be able to help you out."

Wife? "Who? What?"

"Mrs. Claus," she clarified.

"You didn't say anything about a Mrs. Claus."

And he didn't know if the revelation now made things better or worse. On the one hand, he was relieved that he wouldn't have to face a group of kids on his own. On the other, he was skeptical enough about his ability to play a jolly elf, but a jolly elf with a wife?

"I didn't think any kind of warning was necessary," Annie said now. "It was supposed to be me—I was going to be the missus to Dan's Santa, but when he got sick, well, I couldn't leave him to suffer at home alone, so I asked a friend to fill in. But you don't have to worry.

Mrs. Claus will be here to hand out candy canes and keep the line moving—no romantic overtures are required."

"Thanks, I feel so much better now," he said dryly.

"Good," she said, ignoring his sarcasm. "And speaking of spouses—I should get home to my husband, who isn't feeling better but is feeling grateful."

"Do you want me to drop off this costume later?"

"No, I'll come back and get it," she said.

When she'd gone, Bailey chanced a hesitant glance in the mirror. He was afraid he'd look as stupid as he felt—like a kid playing dress-up— and was surprised to realize that he looked like Santa.

There was a brisk knock at the door. "Are you just about ready, Santa?" The scout leader poked his head in the doorway. "Wow, you look great."

"Ho ho ho," Bailey said, testing it out.

The scout leader grinned and gave him two thumbs-up. "The kids are getting restless."

"Mrs. Claus isn't here yet," he said. Although he hadn't originally known there was supposed to be a Mrs. Claus, he now felt at a loss on his own.

"Maybe she got caught up baking cookies at the North Pole," the other man joked.

Whatever she was doing, wherever she was, his missus was nowhere to be found, reminding Bailey of the foolishness of depending on a spouse—even a fictional one.

"Okay, then." He exited the makeshift dressing room and followed the scout leader backstage. Though the curtains were closed, he could hear the excited chatter of what sounded like hundreds, maybe thousands, of children. All of them there to see Santa—and getting stuck with a poor imitation instead.

He felt perspiration bead on his brow and his

hands were clammy inside his white cotton gloves. The leader handed him a big sack filled with candy canes and nodded encouragingly.

It was now or never, and although Bailey would have preferred to go with the never option, he suspected his brother would never forgive him if he chickened out.

Just as he was reaching for the curtain, he heard footsteps rushing up the stage stairs behind him.

Mrs. Claus had arrived.

He didn't have time to give her much more than a cursory glance, noting the floor-length red dress with faux fur trim at the collar and cuffs, and a white apron tied around her waist. Despite the white wig and granny glasses, he could tell that she was young. Her skin was smooth and unwrinkled, her lips plump and exquisitely shaped, and her eyes were as bright and blue as the Montana sky.

"Good, I'm not late." She was breathless, obviously having run some distance, and paused now with her hand on her heart as she drew air into her lungs.

Of course, the action succeeded in drawing his attention to her chest—and the rise and fall of nicely rounded breasts.

"Are you ready to do this?" she asked.

He nodded. *Yes. Please.*

She sent him a conspiratorial wink, and suddenly he felt warm all over. Or maybe it was the bulky costume and the overhead lights that were responsible for the sudden increase in his body temperature.

Then she stepped through the break in the curtains and began to speak to the children.

"Well, we ran into a little bit of rough weather on our way from the North Pole, but we finally made it," she said.

The crowd of children cheered.

Bailey listened to her talk, enjoying the melodic tone of her voice as she set the scene for their audience. He didn't know who she was—he hadn't thought to ask his sister-in-law—but it was immediately apparent to Bailey that Annie had cast a better Mrs. Claus than her husband had a Santa.

"I know you've all been incredibly patient waiting for Santa to arrive and everyone wants to be first in line to whisper Christmas wishes in his ear, but I promise you, it doesn't matter if you're first or last or somewhere in the middle, everyone will have a turn."

They had a wide armchair set up on the stage, beside a decorated Christmas tree surrounded by a pile of fake presents. All he had to do was walk through the curtain and settle into the chair. But his feet were suddenly glued to the floor.

"While Santa finishes settling the reindeer," she said, offering another explanation for the delay of his appearance, "why don't we sing his favorite Christmas song?" She looked out at the audience. "Who knows what Santa's favorite Christmas song is?"

Through the narrow gap between the curtains, he could see hands immediately thrust into the air.

Mrs. Claus listened to several random guesses as the children called for "Jingle Bells," "Let It Snow" and "All I Want for Christmas," shaking her head after each response.

"Okay, I'm going to give you a clue," she said. Then, in a singing voice, she asked, *"Who's got a beard that's long and white?"*

The children responded as a chorus: *"Santa's got a beard that's long and white."*

It was an upbeat and catchy tune with call-and-response lyrics that made it easy for the kids who didn't know the words to sing along anyway, and Bailey found his booted foot tapping against the floor along with the music.

The young audience was completely caught up in the song, and he was reluctant to interrupt. But when Mrs. Claus asked, *"Who very soon will come our way?"* it seemed like an appropriate time to step out from behind the curtain.

"Santa very soon will..."

The response of the chorus faded away as the singers noticed that Santa was, in fact, here now. Several clapped, others pointed and many whispered excitedly to their neighbors.

"And here he is," Mrs. Claus said, then smiled warmly at him and gestured for him to take a seat.

Bailey nodded as he made his way to the chair. He was too nervous to smile back, although she probably couldn't tell if he was or wasn't smiling behind the bushy mustache that hung over his mouth anyway.

He settled into his seat as the leader announced that the young Tiger Scouts would get to visit with Santa first. There were craft tables at the far end of the room for groups waiting to be called and refreshments available.

Bailey felt his palms grow clammy again as the kids lined up, but it didn't take him long to realize that his sister-in-law had been right: the kids knew what they were doing. In fact, most of them didn't expect much from him beyond listening to their wishes and offering them a "Merry Christmas."

There were a lot of requests for specific toys and new video games. A couple of requests for puppies and kittens, building blocks and board games, hockey skates or ballerina slippers. Some of the kids asked questions, wanting to know such random facts as "who's your favorite reindeer?" or "how old is Rudolph?"

He gave vague responses, so as not to contradict anything else they might have been told by their parents, and he was careful not to make any promises, assuring each child only that he would do his best to make their wishes come true.

And if he was a little stiff and unnatural, his supposed wife was the complete opposite— warm and kind and totally believable. She did more than move the line along and hand out candy canes. She seemed to instinctively know what to say and do to put the little ones at ease.

He was about halfway through the Bear Scouts and finally starting to relax into his role when a scowling boy climbed into his lap.

Bailey, anticipating one of the usual requests, was taken aback when the boy said, "Christmas sucks."

"Yeah," Bailey agreed. "Sometimes it does."

Mrs. Claus gasped and the boy's eyes immediately filled with tears.

"You're not s'posed to agree," the child protested. "You're s'posed to tell me that it's gonna be okay."

Since Bailey didn't know what *it* was, he

didn't feel he should make any such promises. But he belatedly acknowledged that he shouldn't have responded the way he did, either. Being called out by the child was only further proof that taking his brother's place as Santa had been a bad idea.

"Now, Santa," Mrs. Claus chided. "I told you not to take your grumpy mood out on the children or I'll have to put *you* on the naughty list."

This threat served to both distract and intrigue the little boy, who eyed her with rapt fascination.

"I'm sorry, Owen," she continued, speaking directly to the child now. "Santa's a little out of sorts today because I warned him that he has to cut down on the cookies if he wants to fit down the chimneys on Christmas Eve."

Then she sent Bailey a pointed look that had him nodding in acknowledgment of her claim as he rubbed his padded belly. "I really like gingerbread," he said, in a conspiratorial whisper to the boy his "wife" had called Owen. "But I definitely don't want to end up on the naughty list."

"Can she do that?" Owen asked.

He nodded again, almost afraid to do otherwise. "So tell me, Owen, is there anything Santa can do to help make the holidays happier for you?"

"Can you make Riley not move to Bozeman?" he asked hopefully.

This time Bailey did shake his head. "I'm sorry."

The child's gaze shifted toward Mrs. Claus again. "Can *she* do it?" Because apparently the boy believed Mrs. Claus not only had authority over her husband but greater magical powers, too.

"I'm sorry," he said again.

Owen sighed. "Then maybe you could leave a PKT-79 under my tree at Christmas and I can give it to Riley, so that he'll have something to remember me by."

It wasn't the first request for a PKT-79, and though Bailey still had no idea what it was, he was touched by the child's request for the gift to give to someone else.

"I'll see what I can do," Santa told him. "Merry Christmas."

"Yeah," Owen said, his tone slightly less glum. "Merry Christmas."

Mrs. Claus held out a candy cane to the boy.

Owen paused to ask her, "You'll make sure Santa can get down my chimney, won't you?"

"You bet I will," she promised, with a wink and a smile for the boy.

Bailey paid more attention after that, to avoid another slipup. When all the children had expressed their wishes to Santa, he and his wife wished everyone a Merry Christmas and headed backstage again.

By the time he made it to the dressing room,

Bailey was more than ready to shed the red coat and everything it represented, but Mrs. Claus walked into the room right behind him.

Closing the door firmly at her back, she faced him with her hands on her hips. "I don't know why anyone would ask someone with such an obviously lousy disposition to play Santa, but you have no right to ruin Christmas for the kids who actually look forward to celebrating the holiday."

Bailey already felt guilty enough for his unthinking response to Owen, but he didn't appreciate being taken to task—*again*—by a stranger, and instinctively lashed out. "A lecture from my loving wife? Now I really do feel like we're married."

"I'd pity any woman who married you," she shot back.

His ready retort stuck in his throat when she took off the granny glasses and removed the wig, causing her long blond hair to tumble over her shoulders, effecting an instant and stunning transformation.

Mrs. Claus was a definite hottie.

Too bad she was also bossy and annoying. And…vaguely familiar looking, he realized.

She twisted her arm up behind her back, trying to reach the top of the zipper, but her fingertips fell short of their target.

While she struggled, Bailey removed his own hat, wig and beard.

She brought her arm around to her front again and tried to reach the back of the dress from over her shoulder, still without success.

He should offer to help. That would be the polite and gentlemanly thing to do. But as his sister-in-law had noted, he was a Grooge and, still stinging from Mrs. Claus's sharp rebuke, not in a very charitable or helpful mood. Instead, he unbuckled his wide belt, removed the heavy jacket and padded belly, eager to shed the external trappings of his own role.

Finally, she huffed out a breath. "You could offer to help, you know?"

"If you need help, you could ask," he countered.

"Would you *please* help me unzip my dress?" she finally said.

"Usually I buy a woman dinner before I try to get her out of her clothes." He couldn't resist teasing. "But since you asked…"

Chapter Two

She turned her back to give Bailey access to the zipper, but not before he saw her roll her eyes in response to his comment. "Do you have to work at being offensive or is it a natural talent?"

"It's a defense mechanism," he said, surprising them both with his honesty. "I screwed up in there—I know I did. I knew I would. That's why I didn't want to put on the stupid suit and pretend to be jolly."

"You ever try actually *being* jolly instead of

just pretending?" she asked, as he tugged on the zipper pull.

"Yeah, but it didn't work out so well."

"I'm sorry." She pulled her arms out of the sleeves and let the bodice fall forward, then stepped out of the skirt to reveal her own clothes: a snug-fitting scoop neck sweater in Christmas red over a pair of skinny jeans tucked into knee-high boots.

A definite hottie with curves that should have warning signs.

He looked away from the danger zone, pushing the suspenders off his shoulders and stepping out of Santa's oversize pants, leaving him clad in a long-sleeve Henley and well-worn jeans. He picked up the flannel shirt he'd shed before donning the Santa coat and put it on over the Henley.

She neatly folded her dress and tucked it into a shopping bag. He watched her out of the corner of his eye, unable to shake the feeling that, though he couldn't think of her name, he was certain he knew her from somewhere.

Before he could ask her if they'd met before, there was a knock at the door.

"Come in."

They both said it at the same time, then she smiled at him, and that easy curve of her lips only increased her hotness factor.

The door opened and Annie poked her head in.

"Oh, Serena, I'm so glad to see that you made it."

"I did. Sorry I was almost late. There was some excitement at the clinic this morning."

Serena.

Clinic.

The pieces finally clicked into place and Bailey realized why the substitute Mrs. Claus looked familiar. She was Serena Langley, a vet tech at the same clinic where his sister-in-law was the receptionist.

"What kind of excitement?" Annie asked, immediately concerned.

"Alistair Warren brought in a fat stray that he found under his porch. The cat turned out not to be fat but pregnant and gave birth to nine kittens."

"Nine?" Annie echoed.

Serena nodded. "Exam Room Three is going to be out of commission for a while, because Brooks doesn't want to disturb the new mom or her babies."

"I can't wait to see them," Annie enthused. "But right now, I want to hear about the substitute Santa's visit with the local scout troop so that I can report back to his more-sick-than-jolly brother."

Bailey turned to Serena again. Truthfully, his gaze had hardly shifted away from her since they'd entered the dressing room. He'd thought it was because he was trying to figure out where they might have crossed paths before, but even with that question now answered, he found his attention riveted on her.

He waited for Serena to say that the substitute Santa had sucked and that the event had been a disaster—although maybe not in terms quite so blunt and harsh. At the very least, he anticipated her telling his sister-in-law that Bailey had screwed up and almost made a kid cry. And he couldn't have disputed either of those points, because they were both true.

But Serena seemed content to let him respond to the inquiry, and he did so, only saying, "It was…an experience."

His sister-in-law's brows lifted. "I'm not sure how to interpret that."

Bailey looked at Mrs. Claus again.

"Everything went well," Serena assured her friend.

Annie exhaled, obviously relieved. "Of course, I knew the two of you would be able to pull it off."

"If you were so confident, you wouldn't have rushed over here to interrogate us," he pointed out. "Although I suspect your concerns were really about Santa and not Mrs. Claus."

"Well, you were the more reluctant substitute," she told him. "Serena didn't hesitate when I asked her to fill in."

"I'm always happy to help a friend," Serena said. "But now I should be on my way."

"What's your hurry?" Annie asked.

"I'm not in a hurry," she denied. "It's just that I left early this morning and…well, you know that Marvin doesn't like it when I'm gone all day."

She seemed a little embarrassed by this admission, or so he guessed by the way her gaze dropped away.

Bailey frowned, wondering about this Marvin and the nature of his relationship with Serena. Was he her husband? Boyfriend? How did he express his disapproval of her absence?

Did he give her the cold shoulder when she got home? Or did he have a hot temper?

The possibility roused his ire. Lord knew he wasn't without faults of his own and tried not to judge others by their shortcomings, but he had no tolerance for men who bullied women or children.

"You worry too much about Marvin," Annie chided.

"You know I can't stand it when he looks at me with those big sad eyes."

"I know you let him use those big sad eyes to manipulate you," Annie said. "You need to stand firm and let him know he's not the boss of you."

Bailey didn't think his sister-in-law should be so quick to disregard her friend's concerns. No one knew what went on behind closed doors of a relationship.

"Is Marvin your...husband?" Bailey asked Serena.

In response to his question, Annie snickered—inappropriately, he thought—and Serena's cheeks flushed with color as she shook her head.

"No, he's my, uh, bulldog."

"Your bulldog," he echoed.

She nodded, the color in her cheeks deepening.

Well, the *big sad eyes* comment made a lot more sense to him now. As the humor of the situation became apparent, he felt his own lips curve.

"He's a rescue," she explained. "And very… needy."

"Only because you let him be," Annie said. "Not to mention that you have a doggy door, so he can go in and out as required."

"Well, yes," Serena admitted. "But he still doesn't like to be alone for too long."

Which led Bailey to believe that there wasn't

anyone else at home—husband or boyfriend—
to put the dog out or deal with his neediness.

Not that it mattered, because he wasn't interested in any kind of romantic relationship with
his sister-in-law's friend and colleague.

Was he?

"I hope Danny is feeling a lot better before
Tuesday," Annie said as she picked up the bags
containing the costumes.

The worry was evident in her friend's voice,
compelling Serena to ask, "What's happening
on Tuesday?"

"We're supposed to play Santa and Mrs.
Claus for a visit to the elementary school."

Which gave Annie's husband only two days
to recuperate from whatever had laid him up.

"I'd be happy to fill in again," Serena immediately offered.

"Oh, that would be wonderful," Annie said.
"And such a weight off my shoulders to not

have to worry about finding a replacement at the last minute again. Thank you both so much."

"Both?" Bailey echoed. "Wait! I never—"

But his sister-in-law didn't pause long enough to allow him to voice any protest. "In that case, I'll leave the costumes with you and just pop over to Daisy's to pick up some soup for Danny. Fingers crossed, he'll be able to keep it down."

"—agreed to anything," he continued.

Of course, Annie was already gone, leaving Serena and Bailey alone again.

She wasn't surprised when he turned toward her, a deep furrow between his brows. "I never agreed to anything," he said again.

"I know, but Annie probably couldn't imagine you'd object to doing a favor for your brother," she said reasonably.

"*Another* favor, you mean."

"Was today really so horrible?"

"That's not the point," he said. "But you're

the type of person who's always the first to volunteer for any task, aren't you?"

She shrugged.

It was true that she hadn't hesitated when Annie asked her to fill in as Mrs. Claus. Although she generally preferred the company of animals to people, she was always happy to help a friend. And when she'd acceded to the request, it had never occurred to her to ask or even wonder about the identity of the man playing Santa Claus.

But even if Annie had told her that it was Bailey Stockton, Serena wouldn't have balked. Because how could she know that she'd have such an unexpected visceral reaction to her friend's brother-in-law?

After all, this was hardly their first meeting. She'd seen him at the clinic—and even once or twice around town, at Crawford's General Store or Daisy's Donut Shop. He was an undeniably handsome man. Of course, as far as she

could tell, all the Stocktons had been geneti-
cally blessed, but there was something about
Bailey that set him apart.

Maybe it was the vulnerability she'd glimpsed
in his eyes. It was the same look of a puppy
who'd torn up the newspaper and only realized after the fact that he'd done something
wrong. Not that she was really comparing
Bailey Stockton to a puppy, but she could tell
that Bailey had felt remorseful as soon as he'd
agreed with Owen's assessment that the holidays sucked.

Serena knew as well as anyone that Christmas wasn't all gingerbread and jingle bells, but
over the years, she'd learned to focus on happy
memories and embrace the spirit of the season.

But now that she and Bailey were no longer
surrounded by kids pumped up on sugar and
excitement about seeing Santa, now that it was
just the two of them, he didn't seem vulnera-

ble at all. He was all man. And every womanly part of her responded to his nearness.

When he'd unzipped her dress, he'd been doing her a favor. There had certainly been nothing seductive about the action. But she'd been aware of his lean hard body behind her, and his closeness had made her heart pound and her knees tremble. And although she was wearing a long-sleeved sweater and jeans beneath the costume, she'd felt the warmth of his breath on the nape of her neck as the zipper inched downward, and a shiver had snaked down her spine.

While she was wearing the costume, she could be Mrs. Claus and play the role she needed to play. But now that the costume had been packed away, she was just Serena Langley again—a woman who didn't know how to chat and flirt with men. In fact, she was completely awkward when it came to interacting with males of the human species, so she decided to do what she always did in uncomfortable situations: flee.

But before she could find the right words to extricate herself, Bailey spoke again.

"And what if I have plans for Tuesday afternoon?" he grumbled. "Not that Annie even considered that possibility."

"If you have plans, then I'll find somebody else to fill in," she said.

In fact, that might be preferable, because being in close proximity to Bailey was stirring feelings…desires…that she didn't want stirred. And while she liked the idea of a boyfriend who might someday turn into a husband, her track record with men was a bunch of false starts and incomplete finishes.

Well, not really a bunch. Barely even a handful. But the number wasn't as important as the fact that, at the end of the day, she was alone.

"Do you have other plans?" she asked.

"No," he reluctantly admitted. "But that's not the point."

"If you don't want to help out, say so," she told him.

"I just don't think I'm the best choice to fill the big guy's boots," he said.

"You managed okay today."

"I'm not sure Owen would agree," he remarked dryly.

"A bump in the road," she acknowledged. "But I'm confident you won't make the same mistake again."

"You're expressing a lot of faith in a guy you don't even know," he warned.

"I'm a pretty good judge of character."

Except that wasn't really true with respect to men. Canines and felines, yes. Even birds and rodents and fish. And while most people would doubt that fish had much character, she'd had a dwarf puffer for four years that had been a true diva in every sense of the word.

"But if you really don't want to do it, that's fine," she said to him now. "I'm sure I can find someone else to play Santa."

And that would probably be a better solution all around, because he was clearly a reluctant Santa and she was reluctant to spend any more time in close proximity to a male who reminded her that she was a woman without a man in her life.

Most of the time, she was perfectly happy with the status quo. But every now and again, she found herself thinking that it might be nice to share her life with someone who could contribute something other than woofs and meows to a conversation. And then she'd force herself to go out and try to meet new people. And her hopes and expectations would be dashed by reality. Again.

But Bailey surprised her by not immediately accepting this offer. "Well, I'm not sure that what I want really matters, since Annie will tell

Dan that I agreed to do it and then, if I don't, I'll have to explain why and how I wriggled my way out of it."

"Are you saying that you *will* do it?" she asked, half hopeful, half wary.

"I guess I am," he agreed.

"Then I guess, unless Dan makes a miraculous recovery, I'll see you at the school on Tuesday."

"Or maybe now," Bailey said, as Serena moved toward the door. Because for reasons he couldn't begin to fathom, he was reluctant to watch her walk away. Or maybe he was just hungry.

She looked at him blankly. "Maybe now what?"

"Maybe I'll see you now—which sounded much better in my head than it did aloud," he acknowledged ruefully. "And which was supposed to be a segue into asking if you wanted to get something to eat."

"Oh." She seemed as uncertain about how to answer the question as he'd been to ask it.

"I was so nervous about the Santa gig that I didn't eat lunch before, and now I'm starving."

Serena offered him a leftover candy cane.

"I think I'm going to want something more than that," he said. "How about you? Are you hungry?"

"Not really."

Her stomach rumbled, calling her out on the fib.

His lips curved. "You want to reconsider your answer?"

"Apparently I am hungry," she acknowledged, one side of her mouth turning up in a half-smile.

"Do you want to grab a bite at the Gold Rush Diner?"

She hesitated.

"It's a simple yes or no question," he told her.

"Like…a date?" she asked cautiously.

"No." His knee-jerk response was as vehement as it was immediate.

Thankfully, Serena laughed, apparently more relieved than insulted by his hasty rejection of the idea.

"In that case, yes," she told him.

Since nothing was too far from anything else in the downtown area of Rust Creek Falls, they decided to leave their vehicles parked at the community center and walk over to the diner. Even on the short walk, the air was brisk with the promise of more snow in the forecast.

The name of the restaurant was painted on the plate-glass front window of the brick building. When Bailey opened the door for Serena, a cowbell overhead announced their arrival.

Though the diner did a steady business, the usual lunch crowd had already cleared out and he gestured for her to choose from the row of vacant booths. She slid across a red vinyl bench and he took a seat opposite her.

After a quick review of the menu, Bailey decided on the steak sub and Serena opted for a house salad.

"Your stomach was audibly rumbling," he reminded her. "I don't think it's going to be satisfied with salad."

"I'm supposed to be going to a dinner and dance at Sawmill Station tonight. The salad will tide me over until then."

"The Presents for Patriots fund-raiser," he guessed. "I've been working with Brendan Tanner on that this year."

"Dr. Smith bought a table and gave the tickets out to his staff."

"Then I'll see you there."

"Unless I decide to stay home with Marvin, Molly and Max."

"I know that Marvin's your dog," he said. "But Molly and Max?"

"Cat and bunny," she admitted.

"You have a lot of pets," he noted.

"Animals are usually better company than people."

"Present company excluded?" he suggested dryly.

Her cheeks flushed. "Maybe it would be more accurate to say that I'm better with animals than with people."

"You were great with the kids today," he assured her.

"Thanks, but kids are generally accepting and easy to please. Especially kids who are focused on something else—such as seeing Santa Claus."

"That reminds me," he said. "What do you know about this PKT-79 all the kids were asking about?"

"It's an upgrade of the 78 that came out in the spring."

"The 78 *what*?"

"An interactive pocket toy that communicates with other similar toys," she explained.

"And where would I find one?" he asked.

"You won't," she told him. "They're sold out everywhere."

"They can't be sold out everywhere," he protested, nodding his thanks to the waitress when she set his plate in front of him.

"It was a headline on my news feed last week—'Must-Have Toy of the Year Sold Out Everywhere.'"

He shook salt over his fries as he considered this setback to his plan.

"Of course, you could always ask Santa for one," she said, tongue in cheek, as she stabbed her fork into a tomato wedge.

"Do Santa's elves have a production line of PKT-79s at the North Pole?"

"They might," she allowed. "The only other option is an aftermarket retailer."

"Like eBay?" he guessed.

She nodded. "But you won't find one reasonably priced," she warned. "Supply and demand."

"I was hoping to get one for Owen," he confided. "To give him a reason to believe that Christmas doesn't suck."

"And because you feel guilty?" she guessed.

"Yeah," he admitted.

"Well, it's a really nice idea," she said. "But I promise you, he'll have a good Christmas even without a PKT-79 under his tree."

"How do you know?"

"Because I know his family, and yes, it's going to suck that his best friend is leaving town after the holidays, but he'll be okay."

"I guess I'll have to take your word for it," Bailey decided. "And since I'm apparently going to do this Santa thing again, I could use some pointers on how to interact with the kids."

"Just try to remember what it was like when you were a kid yourself," she suggested. "Remember the anticipation you felt in those days and weeks leading up to the holiday? All of it finally culminating in the thrill of Christmas morning and the discovery of what Santa left for you under the tree?"

But he didn't want to think about the anticipation leading up to Christmas. He didn't want to think about the holidays at all. Because thinking about the past inevitably brought to mind memories of his parents and all the ways that they'd made the holidays special for their family.

With seven kids to feed and clothe, Christmases were never extravagant, but there were always gifts under the tree—usually something that was needed, such as new work gloves or thermal underwear, and something that was wanted, such as a board game or favorite movie on DVD.

He was so lost in these thoughts—of what he was trying *not* to think about—that he almost forgot he wasn't alone until Serena reached across the table to touch his hand.

The contact gave him a jolt, not just because it was unexpected but because it was somehow both gentle and strong—a woman's touch. And it had been a long time since he'd been touched by a woman.

He deliberately drew his hand away to reach for his soda, sipped. "Remembering those Christmases only serves to remind me of everything I've lost," he told her. "Not that I expect someone like you to understand."

Serena sat back. "What do you mean…someone like me?"

There was a slight edge to her voice that he might have heard if he hadn't been so caught up in his own misery. But because he was and he didn't, he responded without thinking, "Someone who can't know that happiness and joy can turn to grief and despair in an instant."

She reached for her own glass, sipping her

soda before she responded. "You should be careful about making assumptions about other people." Then she meticulously folded her napkin and set it beside her plate. "Thanks for lunch, but I really do need to get home to my pets."

And then, before he could figure out what he'd said or done to put her back up, she was gone.

Chapter Three

By the time she got home, Serena had decided to skip the Presents for Patriots Dinner, Dance & Silent Auction. Though it was barely four o'clock, she'd had a full day already and had no desire to get dressed up and go out. Or it could be that she was looking for an excuse to stay home and avoid seeing Bailey Stockton again.

As she climbed the stairs to her apartment above an accountant's office, the urge to put on a pair of warm fuzzy pajamas and snuggle on the sofa with her pets was strong. And made even stronger when she opened the door and was greeted with so much affection and enthusiasm from Marvin that she couldn't imagine leaving him again.

After giving Marvin lots of ear scratches and an enthusiastic belly rub, she made her way to the bedroom—and found Molly curled up in the center of the bed. She sighed, the exasperated sound alerting the calico to her presence. The cat blinked sleepily.

Serena tried to establish boundaries for her pets—the primary one being that they weren't allowed on her bed unless and until specifically invited. Marvin mostly respected her rules; Max was usually content in his cardboard castle; but Molly roamed freely over the premises.

"Off," she said firmly, gesturing from Molly to the floor.

The calico slowly uncurled herself, yawning as she stretched out, unashamed to have been caught breaking the rules and unwilling to be hurried.

Marvin, having followed Serena into the room, finally noticed Molly on the bed and barked. Molly hissed, as if chastising him for being a tattletale. The dog plopped onto his butt beside Serena and looked up at her with adoring eyes.

"Yes, you're a good boy," she told him.

His tongue fell out of his mouth and he panted happily.

"And you—" She wagged her finger at Molly, then let her hand drop to her side, acknowledging that there was no point in reprimanding an animal who wasn't motivated to do anything but whatever she wanted. As much as the attitude frustrated Serena at times, she couldn't deny that she admired Molly's spirit.

The cat, having made her point, nimbly jumped down off the bed and sauntered toward the door. Marvin started to follow, then turned back to Serena again, obviously torn.

She chuckled softly. "You can go with Molly. I'll be out as soon as I put my jammies on."

But when she opened the closet to put her sweater in the hamper, her gaze was snagged by the dress hanging in front of her.

The dress she'd planned to wear to the Presents for Patriots Dinner, Dance & Silent Auction tonight had been hanging in her closet for eleven months. She'd bought it on sale early in the new year—an after-holiday bargain that she'd been unable to resist—and she'd been excited for the opportunity to finally wear it. Because as much as she usually preferred the company of her animals over that of people, she also enjoyed getting dressed up every once in a while.

She lifted a hand to stroke the crushed velvet fabric. It was the color of rich red wine with a scoop neck, long sleeves and short skirt.

She sighed, silently acknowledging that if she skipped the dinner and dance tonight, it might be another year—or more—before she had the opportunity to wear the dress.

Not to mention that Dr. Brooks Smith's table would already be short two people, as Annie, the clinic receptionist, was at home caring for her sick husband. Which meant that if Serena didn't show, a third meal would go to waste.

But while Annie and Dan would miss the event, Dan's brother would be there—and she wasn't sure if Bailey's attendance was a factor in favor of going or staying home.

When Bailey Stockton left Rust Creek Falls thirteen years ago, he'd thought it was forever. His life and family were gone—torn apart by *his* actions—and he hadn't imagined he would ever want to return. He'd tried to move on with his own life—first in various parts of Wyoming, then in New Mexico—certain he could find a new path. After a few years, he'd even let himself hope that he might make a new family.

That hadn't worked out so well. Though he'd had the best of intentions when he'd exchanged vows with Emily, it turned out that they were just too different—and too stubborn to compromise—which pretty much doomed their marriage from the start.

And then, last December, he'd heard that his brother Luke had made his way back to Rust Creek Falls, and he'd impulsively decided to head in the same direction. He'd arrived in town just in time to witness their brother Danny exchange vows with his high school sweetheart. At the wedding, Bailey had reconnected with most of his siblings, who had persuaded him to stay—at least for a while.

Eleven and a half months later, Bailey was still there. He was living in one of the cabins at Sunshine Farm now and filling most of his waking hours with chores around the ranch. Still, every few weeks he felt compelled to remind himself that he was going to head out again, but the truth was, he had nowhere else to go. And while he'd been certain that he wouldn't ever want to return to the family ranch that held so many memories of the parents they'd lost and the siblings who'd scattered—he'd been wrong about that, too.

When Bailey, Luke and Dan left town, they'd believed the property would be sold by the bank to pay off the mortgages it secured. They'd been shocked to discover that Rob and Lauren Stockton had insurance that satisfied the debts upon their deaths—and even more so to discover that their maternal grandfather had kept up with the property taxes over the years. And while they would all have gladly given up the farm to have their parents back, they were now determined to hold on to the land that was their legacy.

Of course, holding on to the land required a

lot of work—and his brothers had started with the barn, because that was the venue where Dan and Annie had promised to love, honor and cherish one another.

The simple but heartfelt ceremony Bailey had witnessed was very different from the formal church service and elaborate ballroom reception that had marked his own wedding day, but he was confident now that his brother's marriage was destined for a happier fate.

On the day Dan and Annie exchanged their vows, though, Bailey had been much less optimistic about their prospects. Still smarting from the failure of his own union, he'd felt compelled to caution another brother when he saw the stars in Luke's eyes as he'd looked at his date.

Luke and Eva had gone their separate ways for a short while after that. Bailey didn't know if his advice had played a part in that temporary breakup, but he was glad that his brother and new sister-in-law had found their way back to one another. Luke and Eva had gotten engaged last New Year's Eve and married seven months later.

In addition to being committed to one another, they were committed to using Sunshine Farm to spread happiness to others. In fact, Eva's childhood friend Amy Wainwright had recently been reunited with her former—and future—husband, Derek Dalton, at the farm, resulting in the property gaining the nickname Lonelyhearts Ranch.

Bailey couldn't deny that a lot of people were finding love in Rust Creek Falls, including four of his six siblings. But he had no illusions about happily-ever-after for himself. He'd already been there, done that and bought the T-shirt—then lost the T-shirt in his divorce.

But he was happy to help out with Presents for Patriots. He would even acknowledge that he enjoyed working with Brendan Tanner—

because the retired marine didn't try to get into his head or want to talk about his feelings, which was more than he could say about his siblings.

Bailey believed wholeheartedly in the work of Presents for Patriots. He had the greatest respect for the sacrifices made by enlisted men and women and was proud to participate in the community's efforts to let the troops know they were valued and appreciated. Maybe sending Christmas gifts was a small thing, but at least it was something, and Bailey was pleased to be part of it.

He was less convinced of the value of this dinner and dance. Sure, it was a fund-raiser for a good cause, but Bailey suspected that most of the guests would be couples, and—as the only single one of his siblings currently living in Rust Creek Falls—he was already tired of feeling like a third wheel.

Not that he wanted to change his status. No,

he'd learned the hard way that he was better off on his own. No one to depend on and no one depending on him. But it was still awkward to be a single man in a social gathering that was primarily made up of couples.

He looked around the crowd gathered at Sawmill Station, hoping to see Serena in attendance. She'd said that she had a ticket for the event, but considering the abruptness with which she'd left the restaurant after lunch, he had to wonder if she'd changed her mind about coming.

Her plans shouldn't matter to him. After all, he barely knew her. But he couldn't deny there was something about her—even when she was admonishing him for his admittedly inappropriate behavior—that appealed to him.

In fact, while she'd been scolding him, he'd had trouble understanding her words because his attention had been focused on the movements of her mouth. And he'd found himself wondering if those sweetly curved lips would stop moving if he covered them with his own—or if they'd respond with a matching passion.

Yeah, he barely knew the woman, but he knew that he wanted to kiss her—and that realization made him wary. It had been a lot of years since he'd felt such an immediate and instinctive attraction to a woman, and he would have happily lived out the rest of his days without experiencing that feeling again. Because he knew now that the euphoric feeling didn't last—and when it was gone, his heart might suffer more dings and dents.

So it was probably for the best that she'd walked out of the diner before he'd had a chance to ask her to be his date tonight. Because while he wasn't entirely comfortable being a single man surrounded by couples, at least he didn't have to worry about the stirring of unexpected desires—and the even more dangerous yearnings of his heart.

Just when he'd managed to convince himself that was true, he turned away from the bar with a drink in hand and saw her. And his foolish heart actually skipped a beat.

The silky blond hair that had spilled over her shoulders when she'd removed the Mrs. Claus wig was gathered up on top of her head now. Not in a tight knot or a formal twist, but a messy—and very sexy—arrangement of curls. Several loose strands escaped the knot to frame her face.

She was wearing a dress. The color was richer and deeper than red, and the fabric clung to her mouthwatering curves. The skirt of the dress ended just above her knees, and she wore pointy-toed high-heeled shoes on her feet.

He took a few steps toward her and noticed that there were sparkles in her hair. Crystal snowflakes, he realized, as he drew nearer. She'd made up her face, too. Not that she needed any artificial enhancement, but the long lashes that surrounded her deep blue eyes were now thicker and darker, and her temptingly curved lips were slicked with pink gloss.

"You look… Wow," he said, because he couldn't find any other words that seemed adequate.

Her cheeks flushed prettily. "Back atcha."

He knew his basic suit and bolero tie were nothing special, particularly in this crowd, but he smiled, grateful that she didn't seem to be holding a grudge. "I wasn't sure you were going to come."

"Neither was I," she admitted.

"I'm glad you did," he told her. "And I hope you brought your checkbook—there's a lot of great stuff on the auction table."

"As soon as I figure out where I'm sitting for dinner, I'll take a look," she promised.

"You can sit with me," he invited.

"I think I'm supposed to be at Dr. Smith's table."

He shook his head. "There are no assigned tables."

She looked toward the dining area, where long wooden tables were set in rows on either side of the dance floor.

The decor was festive but simple. Of course, Brendan and Bailey had left all those details in the hands of the event planners, who had adorned the tables with evergreen branches and holly berries, with tea lights in clear glass bowls at the center of each grouping of four place settings. The result was both festive and rustic, perfect for the venue and the occasion.

"I've never been here before," Serena confided. "But this place is fabulous. You and Brendan did a great job."

Bailey immediately shook his head. "This was all Caroline Ruth and her crew. The only thing me and Brendan can take credit for is putting her in charge," he said. "And picking the food."

"What will we be eating tonight?" she asked.

He plucked a menu off a nearby table and read aloud: "Country biscuits with whipped butter, mixed greens with poached pears, candied walnuts and a honey vinaigrette, grilled hand-carved flat iron steak, red-skin mashed potatoes and blackened corn, with huckleberry pie or chocolate mousse for dessert."

"And that's why I had salad for lunch," she told him.

He chuckled as he steered her toward the table where Luke and Eva were already seated, along with Brendan Tanner and his fiancée, Fiona O'Reilly, and Fiona's sister Brenna and her husband, Travis Dalton.

Conversation during dinner covered many and various topics—Presents for Patriots, of course, including the upcoming gift-wrapping at the community center—but Brendan and Fiona's recent engagement was also a subject of much interest and discussion.

"So how long have you and Serena been dating?" Brenna asked, as she dipped her spoon into her chocolate mousse.

Bailey looked up, startled by the question. "What?"

Serena paused with her wineglass halfway to her lips, obviously taken aback, as well.

"I asked how long you've been dating," Brenna repeated.

"They're not dating," Eva responded to the question first. "But they're married."

"Really?" Brenna sounded delighted and intrigued by this revelation.

"Not really," Serena said firmly.

"I don't know." Eva spoke up again, winking at Bailey and Serena to let them know she was teasing. "There were a lot of people at the community center today who believe you are."

Serena rolled her eyes. "Only because we were dressed up as Santa and Mrs. Claus."

"There's nothing wrong with a little role-playing to spice things up in the bedroom," Brenna asserted.

Serena shook her head, her cheeks redder than the dress she'd worn during their role-playing that afternoon. "I should have stayed home tonight."

"I'm just teasing you," Brenna said, immediately contrite. "Although Travis and I fell in love for real while we were only pretending to be engaged."

"I cheered for both of you on *The Great Roundup*," Serena admitted.

"Then you saw me win the grand prize," Travis chimed in.

Bailey frowned. Though reality shows weren't his thing, it would have been impossible to be in Rust Creek Falls the previous year and not follow the events that played out when two local residents were vying for the big money on the television show. "It was Brenna who won the million dollars."

"That's true," Travis confirmed, sliding an arm across his wife's shoulders and drawing her into his embrace. "But I won Brenna."

She smiled up at him. "And I won you."

"And I need some air," Bailey decided.

"Me, too," Serena said, pushing back her chair.

They exited the main reception area but didn't venture much farther than that. Leaving the building would require collecting their coats and bundling up against the frigid Montana night.

"They don't mean to be obnoxious," Bailey said when he and Serena were alone. "At least, I don't think they do."

She laughed softly. "I didn't think they were obnoxious. I thought they were adorable."

"Really?"

"Yeah. I mean, I watched *The Great Roundup,* but you never know how much of those reality shows is real, how much is staged, how much is selectively edited. It's nice to see that they truly are head over heels in love with one another."

"For now," Bailey remarked.

Serena frowned. "You don't think they'll last?"

He shrugged. "I don't think the odds are in their favor."

"Love isn't about odds," she said. "It's a leap of faith."

"A leap that frequently ends with one or both parties hitting the ground with a splat."

"Spoken like someone who has some experience with the splat," she noted.

He nodded. "Because I do."

"Of course, most people don't make it through life without a few bumps and bruises."

"Bumps and bruises usually heal pretty easily," he said.

Bailey's matter-of-fact statement told Serena that the heartbreak he'd experienced had left some pretty significant scars. She also suspected that the romance gone wrong had reopened wounds caused by the loss of his parents and the separation from his family when he was barely more than a teenager.

"Usually," she agreed.

"I'm sorry," he said, after another moment had passed.

The spontaneous and unexpected apology surprised her. "Why are you sorry?"

"Because I obviously said something that upset you at lunch today."

"I can be overly sensitive at times," she admitted.

"Does that mean I'm forgiven?" he asked hopefully.

She nodded. "You're forgiven."

"That's a relief," he told her. "We wouldn't want the kids of Rust Creek Falls Elementary School to worry about any obvious tension between Santa and Mrs. Claus."

"I'm not sure they care about Santa's marital

status so long as he delivers their presents on Christmas Eve."

"Which he wouldn't be able to do if the missus got possession of the sleigh and custody of the reindeer in the divorce," Bailey pointed out.

"Then he better do everything he can to keep her happy," she suggested.

"If Santa had a secret formula for keeping a woman happy, it would top every man's Christmas list," he said.

"Ha ha."

"I'm not joking," he assured her. "But in the interests of keeping you happy, can I buy you a drink?"

"No, thanks. I had a glass of wine with dinner and that's my limit."

"One glass?"

She nodded.

"Okay, how about a dance?"

"The words sound like an invitation," she

remarked. "But the tone suggests that you're hoping the offer will be declined."

"Maybe, for your sake, I'm hoping it will," he said. "Because I'm not a very good dancer."

"Then why did you ask?"

He shrugged. "Because it might seem like everyone else is paired off, but I have noticed that there are a few single guys in attendance and I know they're just waiting for me to turn my back for a second so they can move in on you."

"Should I be flattered? Or should I get out my pepper spray?"

"Maybe you should just dance with me," he suggested.

So Serena took the hand he proffered and let him lead her to the dance floor. But the minute he took her in his arms, she knew that her acquiescence had been a mistake. Being close to him, she felt those unwanted feelings stir again.

She'd had a few boyfriends in her twenty-five years, and even a couple of lovers, but she'd never really been in love. And though she didn't know much about Bailey, the intensity of the attraction she felt for him warned her that he might be the man she finally and completely fell for.

But she also knew that he didn't want to be that man, and his brief and blunt comments about his marriage gone wrong should serve as a warning to her. Which was too bad, because she really liked being in his arms. And notwithstanding his claim that he wasn't a good dancer, he moved well.

As the last notes of the song trailed away, she tipped her head back to look at him.

The heels she wore added three inches to her height, so that if he lowered his head just a little, his mouth would brush against hers.

She really wanted him to kiss her.

But they were barely more than strangers and in a very public setting. And yet, in that moment, everyone and everything else faded into the background so that there was only the two of them.

Then he did tip his head, so that his mouth hovered a fraction of an inch above hers. And she held her breath, waiting...

A guitar riff blasted through the air—an abrupt change of tempo for the couples on the dance floor—and the moment was lost.

Serena stepped back. "I—I'm going to check out the auction items."

So Bailey returned to the table without her.

"Watching you and Serena on the dance floor, I could see why Brenna thought that you guys were together," Luke commented.

"Why were you watching us instead of dancing with your wife?" Bailey asked his brother.

"Because I was working at Daisy's at 4:00 a.m.," Eva responded to the question. "And my feet are very happy to *not* be dancing right now.

But he's right," she continued. "You and Serena look good together."

"Except that we're not together," he reminded his brother and sister-in-law.

They exchanged a glance.

"Denial," Eva said.

Luke nodded.

"Look, it's great that the two of you found one another and happiness together, but not everyone else in the world wants the same thing," Bailey told them.

"You mean they're not ready to admit that they want the same thing," Eva said.

Bailey just shook his head.

"A year ago, I was a skeptic, too," Luke said. "And then I met Eva."

The smile she gave her husband was filled with love and affection. And maybe it did warm Bailey's heart to see Luke and Eva so happy. And Danny and Annie. And Jamie and Fallon.

And his sister Bella and Hudson. And maybe he was just the tiniest bit envious.

But only the tiniest bit—not nearly enough to be willing to risk putting his own heart on the line again.

Thankfully, he was saved from responding by the sound of—

"Is that dogs barking the tune of 'Jingle Bells'?" Eva asked.

"That's gotta be Serena's phone," Bailey noted.

Luke picked it up from the table, his brows lifting when he looked at the case. Then he turned it around so Eva and Bailey could see the image of a bulldog wearing a Santa hat.

Bailey wasn't going to judge her for loving Christmas as much as she loved her dog, especially when the call had provided a timely interruption to an increasingly awkward conversation. He took the phone from his brother and went to find Serena.

"This would send Marvin into a frenzy of joy," she told him, gesturing with the pen in her hand to a Canine Christmas basket filled with toys and treats that had been donated by Brooks Smith and his wife, Jazzy.

Bailey glanced at the bid sheet. "Looks like there's already a bidding war between Paige Traub and Lissa Christensen."

"And now me, too," she said, as she scrawled her offer on the page.

He lifted his brows at the number she'd written. "You doubled the last bid."

"It's for a good cause," she reminded him.

"So it is," he agreed.

"Is there anything here that's caught your eye?" she asked.

He knew she was referring to the auction table, but the truth was, he hadn't been able to take his eyes off *her* since she'd arrived.

"I'm still looking," he told her. But as he'd

very recently reminded his brother and sister-in-law, he wasn't looking for happily-ever-after.

"There's a lot to look at," she said. "Everything from kids' toys and knitted baskets to a weekend getaway at Maverick Manor." She sighed. "Unfortunately, the bids on that are already out of my price range."

And yet she was willing to overpay for some dog toys to support a good cause and make Marvin happy.

"Is this Marvin?" he asked, holding up her phone.

She smiled. "No, it's a stock photo, but I bought the case because it looks a lot like him."

"Well, you might want to check your messages," he said. "Because you missed a call."

Serena finished writing her contact information on the bid sheet, then took her phone from him. "I can't imagine who might be calling me. Almost everyone I know is here tonight," she told him, as she unlocked the screen with her thumbprint.

He was surprised to see her expression change as she scanned the message. The light in her eyes dimmed, her lips thinned. She texted a quick response, then said, "I have to go."

"Now? Why?"

"My mom's at the Ace in the Hole."

"And?"

She just shook her head. "Long story."

"Do you want me to come with you?" he asked.

She seemed surprised that he would offer. "No," she said, but softened the rejection with a smile. "I appreciate the offer, but it's not necessary."

He took her phone from her again, then added his name and number to her list of contacts. "Just in case you change your mind."

"Thanks," she said, and even managed another smile. But he could tell that her mind was

already at the bar and grill down the street—
and whatever trouble he suspected was waiting for her there.

Chapter Four

Serena found a vacant spot in the crowded lot outside the Ace in the Hole and shifted into Park. She pocketed the keys as she exited her vehicle, the sick feeling in the pit of her stomach increasing with every step she took closer to the oversize ace of hearts playing card that blinked in neon red over the front door. She could hear the music from the jukebox inside as she climbed the two rough-hewn wooden steps. The price of beer was subject to regular increases, but the ancient Wurlitzer still played three songs for a quarter.

There were a few cowboys hanging around outside, cigarettes dangling from their fingers or pursed between their lips. She held her breath as she walked through their cloud of smoke and ignored the whistles and crude remarks tossed in her direction as she reached for the handle of the old screen door with its rusty hinges.

Once inside, her gaze immediately went to the bar that ran the length of one wall with stools lined up along it. Booths hugged the other walls, with additional tables and chairs crowded around the perimeter of the dance floor.

She made a cursory scan of the bodies perched on the stools at the bar. The mirrored wall behind the rows of glass bottles allowed her to see their faces. She recognized many, but none belonged to her mother.

Rosey Traven, the owner of the Ace, was pouring drinks behind the bar. Catching Serena's eye, she tipped her head toward the back. Serena forced her reluctant feet to move in that direction.

She found her mother seated across from a man that Serena didn't recognize. A friend? A date? A stranger?

Amanda Langley mostly kept to herself. For the past couple of years, she'd worked as an admin assistant at the mill, but outside of her job, she didn't have a lot of friends. And as far as Serena knew, she didn't date much, either.

She was an attractive woman, with the same blond hair and blue eyes as her daughter, but a more boyish figure and a raspy voice courtesy of a fifteen-year pack-a-day habit that she'd finally managed to kick a few years earlier.

The man seated across from her wasn't bad looking, either. He had broad shoulders, a shaven—or maybe bald—head, and a beard and moustache that were more salt than pepper.

Serena hesitated, trying to decide whether to advance or retreat, when her mother glanced up and saw her. Amanda looked surprised at first—and maybe a little guilty? Then she smiled and beckoned her daughter over.

Serena made her way through the crowd to the table.

"Rena—what are you doing here?"

She bent her head to kiss her mother's cheek. "I think the more important question is what are *you* doing here?"

"I'm having dinner with…a friend."

Serena looked again at the man seated across the table. Up close, she could see that his twinkling eyes were blue and his good humor was further reflected in the easy curve of his lips. She added well-mannered to her assessment when he stood up and offered his hand. "Mark Kesler."

She took it automatically. "Serena Langley."

"It's a pleasure to finally meet you, Serena," he said. "Your mother's told me so much about you."

"That's interesting, because she's told me absolutely nothing about you."

"Serena." Her name was a sharp rebuke from her mother.

But Mark only chuckled. "It's okay, Amanda. In fact, it's nice to know that your daughter looks out for you."

"Is that what you're doing, Serena?" her mother asked.

"I can't seem to help myself," she admitted.

Because it was warm in the bar, she unwound the scarf from around her neck and unbuttoned her coat. Then she reached across the table to pick up her mother's glass and tipped it to her lips.

"If you want a drink, you can order your own soda," Amanda said dryly.

"I just wanted a sip," she said.

"And did that sip satisfy your…thirst?"

They both knew that what her mother really meant was *curiosity*, but Serena refused to feel guilty for needing to know what was in her mother's glass. And she wasn't going to apologize, either.

"As a matter of fact, it did," she said.

Amanda picked up a fry from her plate, nibbled on it. Then she said quietly, "Mark knows I'm an alcoholic."

The man in question reached into his jacket pocket and pulled out a coin, then slid it across the table for Serena to look at.

She immediately recognized it as a sobriety coin. Her mother had recently earned one with the Roman numeral V on it, commemorating five years without a drink. The numerals inside the circle inside the triangle of this coin read XXV.

"I understand, more than most, that sobriety is a daily challenge for addicts," he told her.

"Then why would you bring her here?" she wanted to know.

"Because the Ace has the best burgers in town," Mark said.

Serena couldn't deny that, but she still worried about her mother's ability to resist the temptation that beckoned from the assortment of bottles lined up behind the bar. Gin had always been Amanda's preferred poison, but beggars weren't usually choosers, and for a lot of years, she drank anything she could get her hands on.

"But I forgot how much food they give you here," Amanda said now. "And while I managed to finish the burger, I barely touched my fries." She nudged the plate toward her daughter.

Serena shook her head, declining the silent offer. "I ate at the Presents for Patriots event."

"That's why you're all dressed up," her mother realized. "Did you go with a date?"

"No." But she thought about Bailey now—about how much she'd enjoyed chatting with him during the meal. And how much she'd savored the security of his strong arms around her on the dance floor, and the heat of his lean hard body close to hers, stirring long-dormant desires inside her.

But sitting at the same table and sharing a single dance didn't make a chance encounter a date. Maybe if he'd kissed her... And for a brief moment at the end of the song, she'd thought he might. But he didn't.

"Oh," Amanda said, obviously disappointed by her daughter's response. Then to *her* date, she said, "If Serena spent a little less time with animals and a little more with people, she might find a nice young man to settle down with."

"Maybe she doesn't want to settle down," Mark suggested.

"Thank you," Serena said, grateful for his acknowledgment of the possibility.

It wasn't the truth, of course. She *did* want to settle down—but she had no intention of settling. She wanted to fall in love with a man who loved her just as much, then get married and raise a couple of kids and grow old together.

"She wants a husband and a family," Amanda insisted, as if privy to her daughter's innermost thoughts. "But she has some trust issues that get in the way of her getting too close to anyone. Totally my fault," she acknowledged ruefully.

"Not totally," Serena said, because she couldn't deny that her childhood experiences continued to influence her expectations of adult relationships. "My father bears equal responsibility for walking out on both of us."

"And then I made things worse."

"I don't think there's anything to be gained

by assigning blame," Mark protested, reaching across the table to cover Amanda's hand with his own, a tangible gesture of his support.

"Step Five—admitting the nature of our mistakes."

Mark started to say something else, but his attention was snagged by the vibration of his cell phone on the table. He glanced at the screen, then at Amanda. "I'm sorry but—"

"Go," she said. "You don't need to apologize, just go."

"Excuse me," he said to Serena, as he slid out of the booth, already connecting the call.

"Mark is an active AA sponsor," Amanda explained when the man in question had moved out of earshot.

"Is that how the two of you met?" Serena asked.

"We met at a meeting," her mother confirmed. "But he was never my sponsor."

"But he was an alcoholic," she noted.

"*Is* an alcoholic. Sober for more than twenty-five years, but still an alcoholic."

Serena nodded. Aside from her own experience with Amanda, she'd attended enough Al-Anon meetings as the daughter of an alcoholic to know that the battle against addiction was ongoing.

She also knew that her mother had worked hard to get and stay sober, and she deserved credit for that. "I'm sorry I overreacted," she said now.

"I'm sorry, too," Amanda said. "Because I know you have valid reasons to be concerned."

"Mark seems nice," she acknowledged.

"And you're worried that if I get emotionally involved and it doesn't work out, I'm going to lose myself in the bottle again?" her mother guessed.

Serena didn't—couldn't—deny it, so she remained silent.

"We both worried about the same thing,"

Amanda confided. "It's why we fought against our feelings for one another for so long."

"How long have you known him?" she asked curiously.

"Twelve years."

Her brows lifted. "How long have you been dating?"

"We've been spending more and more time together over the past few years, but tonight was our first official date," her mother told her.

"And your daughter crashed it."

Amanda smiled. "I'm always glad to see you."

It was a sincere statement, not a commentary on the scarcity of their visits, but she felt a twinge of guilt nevertheless. Over the past five years, her mother had made a lot of efforts and overtures that Serena had resisted—not as punishment or payback, but simply out of self-preservation.

She'd lost track of the number of times that

she'd given her mother "one more chance" to be the mother that she wanted her to be, and somewhere along the line, she'd stopped believing that Amanda could ever be that person. Now, however, Serena acknowledged that she hadn't always been the daughter that her mother wanted her to be, and maybe it was time to work toward changing that.

When Mark finished his phone call and came back to the table, Serena wished them both a good-night and headed out. She caught Rosey's eye again as she passed the bar and gave the other woman a thumbs-up. Rosey nodded and continued to pour beer.

The time displayed on the Coors Light clock on the wall assured Serena that it wasn't too late to go back to the dinner and dance—and check on her bids—but her emotions were raw and she didn't think it was wise to seek out the company of a man whose mere presence churned her up inside.

No, the smart thing to do would be to go home to the animals who would shower her with unconditional love—or, in Molly's case, tolerant affection.

So resolved, she buttoned her coat up to her throat and braced herself for the slap of cold as she walked through the door and into the night. A different group of smokers huddled outside now—willingly braving the frigid air for a hit of nicotine.

Serena kept her head down and moved briskly toward her vehicle, parked at the far edge of the lot. As she drew nearer, she saw a tall broad-shouldered figure leaning against the tailgate of the truck in the slot beside her SUV.

She thought about the guys who'd been hanging around outside when she arrived and wondered—with more than a little bit of trepidation—if one of them had decided to wait by her vehicle until she came out again.

Her heart pounded against her ribs, and she

considered going back into the bar and asking Mark to escort her to her SUV. Instead, she drew in a steadying breath and slipped her hand into her pocket to retrieve her keys. She held them in her fist, so that the pointed ends protruded between her knuckles as her grandmother had taught her to do, and walked purposefully, projecting more confidence than she felt.

Though the figure was mostly in shadow, as she got closer, she sensed that there was something familiar about his shape.

"Bailey?"

He turned, and the light in the distance provided enough illumination of his profile to confirm that her guess was correct. Her heart continued to hammer against her ribs, though its frantic rhythm was no longer inspired by fear but relief—and pleasure.

"I know you didn't call, but I also know that the crowd here can get a little rowdy on week-ends, and I wanted to make sure you were okay," he said, answering her unspoken question.

"I'm okay," she assured him.

"Do you want to talk?"

"No," she replied automatically, having grown accustomed to dealing with everything on her own since her grandmother had retired down to Arizona three years earlier. Then she reconsidered. "Maybe."

"We could go back inside to have a drink," he suggested.

She shook her head. "Definitely not."

His brows lifted.

"I wouldn't say no to hot cocoa at Daisy's, though."

"Hot cocoa at Daisy's it is," he agreed.

Daisy's Donut Shop was practically a landmark in Rust Creek Falls. Originally renowned for the best coffee—and the only donuts—in town, the owner had eventually responded to the demand for a wider range of food options. As a result, Daisy's menu now included a rotating selection of soups and sandwiches, but it was the mouthwatering sweets on display in the glass-fronted cases that continued to draw and tempt the most customers.

There were several people lined up at the counter ahead of them when they arrived.

"I think we came in with the last of the movie crowd," Serena noted.

Bailey had almost forgotten that movies were shown at the high school on Friday and Saturday nights—but only so long as the Wildcats didn't have the gymnasium booked for a game, in which case the bleachers would be filled with residents cheering on the local team.

"Waiting in line gives us more time to check out the desserts Eva made today," he said, gesturing to the glass-fronted cases.

Of course, it was late, and the offerings that remained were limited—but still tempting.

"Just a regular hot cocoa for me," Serena said, stepping up to the counter.

Bailey looked dubious. "Just regular hot cocoa, like you could make for yourself at home?"

She shook her head. "I've tried all kinds of hot cocoa mixes. I've even tried making it from scratch, but it's never as good as Daisy's."

"Secret recipe," the server said with a wink.

"Coffee, decaf, for me," Bailey said. "And I've got to have one of those cheesecake-stuffed snickerdoodles."

"Didn't you already have dessert at Sawmill Station?" Serena asked him. "In fact, I'm pretty sure you ate your chocolate mousse and finished your sister-in-law's huckleberry pie."

"I did," he confirmed. "But that was more than two hours ago."

She smiled as she shook her head.

"Anything else for you?" the server asked.

"No, thanks," Serena said.

"Whipped cream and chocolate drizzle on your cocoa?"

"Mmm, yes," she agreed.

When they were seated with their hot beverages—and Bailey's enormous cookie—Serena wrapped her hands around her mug and announced, "My mother's an alcoholic."

"Ahh," he said, understanding now why she'd raced away from the silent auction when she learned that her mother was at the town's notorious drinking hole. "Was she...drunk?"

Serena shook her head. "She was drinking diet cola and eating a cheeseburger."

"Strange place to go for a diet cola," he noted.

"Best place in town for a burger."

Now she nodded.

"So why are you all wound up?"

She couldn't deny that she was. Not when her hands were clutching her mug like it was a buoy keeping her afloat in stormy seas—but maybe that was an apt analogy for her life at the moment.

"I can't help it," she admitted. "I get a message like that, and the memories—years and years of horrible memories—play through my head like a horror movie on fast-forward."

"Who told you that she was there?"

"Rosey made the original call. Then Shelby sent a text when I was already on my way."

"I don't think I know a Shelby," he said.

"She used to be Shelby Jenkins, but she married Dean Pritchett a few years back," she told him. "She's worked at the Ace for a long time and has good instincts about people—and knows which customers to keep an eye on."

"Gives a whole new meaning to neighborhood watch," he remarked.

"Over the years, Rosey and Shelby have had a front-row seat to some of my mother's struggles—and mine," she explained. "And five years of sobriety hasn't helped me forget more than a decade of drinking."

His brows lifted.

She sighed. "And I guess two years of weekly therapy didn't quite succeed in helping me work through my anger and frustration and fear."

"That's why you wouldn't have more than one glass of wine tonight," he guessed.

She nodded. "Some scientists believe there's a genetic component to addiction, and I don't want to take any chances. Although—" she lifted her mug "—it wouldn't be wrong to say that I'm addicted to chocolate."

Then she sipped her cocoa, ending up with a whipped cream moustache that she swiped away with a stroke of her tongue.

The gesture drew Bailey's attention to the temptation of her mouth again, and he silently chided himself for not taking advantage of the opportunity he'd had to kiss her when they were on the dance floor.

But that opportunity had passed, and he owed her the courtesy of paying attention to what she was saying without being distracted by his own fantasies.

Except that a tiny bit of whipped cream clung to the indent at the center of her top lip, and it was driving him to distraction. He finally reached across the table and brushed his thumb over her lip, wiping away the cream.

He heard her sharp intake of breath, watched her eyes widen with awareness. And maybe… arousal?

Or maybe he was projecting.

"Whipped cream," he explained.

"Oh." She reached for her napkin and wiped her mouth. "I probably should have skipped the whipped cream and chocolate sauce—they're messy."

"There's nothing wrong with messy," he told

her, imagining that they could have a lot of fun getting messy together with whipped cream and chocolate sauce.

Serena blushed, making him wonder if her thoughts had gone in the same direction as his own.

There was definitely a zing in the air—a sizzle of attraction that ratcheted up the temperature about ten degrees whenever he was with her.

He'd been back in Rust Creek Falls for almost a year, and during that time, he'd crossed paths with any number of undeniably attractive women. Several had flirted with him, a few had offered more than a phone number, but he hadn't been tempted by any of them.

But after only a few hours with Serena Langley, he hadn't been able to get her out of his mind. When she'd left the Gold Rush Diner earlier that day, he'd counted the hours until the fund-raiser in anticipation of seeing her there. And when she'd excused herself from that event, he could tell she was upset about something. And because he'd worried about an attractive single woman walking into a place like the Ace alone, he'd followed her, just to make sure she was okay.

Now he was sitting across from her at Daisy's Donut Shop, watching her sip hot cocoa and trying to resist the temptation to imagine her naked. He was feeling better about life, the universe and everything than he'd felt in a very long time—maybe even since he'd left Rust Creek Falls following the deaths of his parents thirteen years earlier. Which confirmed a crucial fact: Serena Langley was a dangerous woman. And if he wasn't careful, her sparkling eyes, warm smile and open heart could pose a significant threat to the walls he'd deliberately built around his own damaged vessel.

So he would be careful, he resolved. He would take a step back—maybe several steps—

to avoid the danger of another emotional splat. But those steps could wait until tomorrow, he decided, as he popped the last bite of snickerdoodle into his mouth.

Because tonight, he was really enjoying being with her.

Chapter Five

"I know, I know," Serena said, as she kicked off her shoes inside the door. "I promised I wouldn't be late, but I got caught up."

Marvin didn't move from the spot where he'd been sitting when she opened the door, his big sad eyes filled with silent reproach.

"I'm sorry," she said, crouching down to rub his ears.

He closed his eyes, savoring her touch.

Then she sighed. "Actually, that's a lie. I'm sorry you missed me, but I'm not sorry I'm late, because I had a really good time with Bailey tonight."

Marvin tilted his head.

"Am I forgiven?" she asked, continuing to scratch where he liked it best.

His licked her hand.

"Thank you," she said, and kissed the top of his head before rising to her feet again and moving toward the bedroom to change.

On the way, she checked on Max, who was sleeping soundly in his bed. She found Molly curled up on *her* bed again, but Serena pretended she didn't see her there, because attempting to reprimand the stubborn calico only proved to both of them that the cat was the one calling the shots.

Instead, Serena hung her dress back up in the closet and finally donned the warm fuzzy pajamas that had beckoned to her hours earlier. After brushing her teeth, she wanted nothing more than to climb beneath the covers of her bed, but she felt guilty for neglecting Marvin through most of the day and night, so she returned to the living room. She played some tug-of-war with him and his favorite knotted rope, then a few minutes of fetch—he'd always been good at finding and retrieving the ball, but not so good at returning it to her.

When he finally tired of the game and crawled into her lap, she lifted her hand to his head to rub his ears, and he sighed contentedly and closed his eyes.

"I think I'm developing a serious crush," Serena confided to her pet.

He opened one eye, as if to assure her that he was listening.

She smiled as she continued to stroke his short glossy fur.

"I know it's crazy," she admitted. "I barely know the guy. And yet…there's just something about him.

"Or maybe it's just been so long since I've

spent any time with a man that I'm making this into more than it is. I mean, it wasn't even a date—we just both happened to be at the same event. But it felt like a date. And it was so nice to talk to a guy who seemed to listen to what I was saying.

"Of course, you're a good listener, too, but sometimes it's nice to talk to someone who actually talks back."

Marvin responded with a low growl.

She laughed softly. "I'm not denying that you know how to communicate," she said, attempting to placate her pet. "But we really don't share a dialogue. And, if I'm being completely honest, I like to look at him, too. Because Bailey Stockton is hot. And the way he looks at me, I feel like I'm more than a vet tech or a pet owner or 'the girl who lives upstairs,' as Mr. Harrington calls me. I feel attractive and desirable, and I haven't felt that way in a long time."

Marvin tilted his head to lick her hand.

"I know you love me," she said. "And I love you. But as sweet as your doggy kisses are, they don't compare to real kisses. At least, I don't think they do. Of course, it's been so long since I've been kissed by a man, I can't be sure."

But there had been that almost-kiss moment, during which she'd experienced so much joyful anticipation she was certain that sharing a real kiss with Bailey Stockton would make her toes curl inside her shoes.

"And even though I was gone all night, I was thinking about you," Serena told Marvin. "And hopefully my bid on the— Well, I can't tell you what it was, because if my bid was successful, it will be your Christmas present and I wouldn't want to ruin the surprise. Anyway, tomorrow I will be home all day," she promised. "Maybe I'll even make some of your favorite treats."

Marvin's head lifted at the last word, and she laughed again.

"And, because you sometimes get too many *t-r-e-a-t-s,* we'll go for a nice long walk."

He immediately dropped his head again and closed his eyes, faking sleep so he could pretend he hadn't heard her.

"People told me to get a dog, they said I'd be more active. I swear, I got the only dog on the planet that's even lazier than me," Serena lamented. "But a walk will do both of us good—and I definitely need one because I had hot cocoa with whipped cream and chocolate sauce tonight."

And her lips tingled as she recalled the sensation of Bailey's thumb brushing over her lip to wipe away a remnant of the cream.

She pushed the tempting memory aside and refocused her attention on Marvin, who continued to fake sleep.

"I know you don't love to walk in the winter," she acknowledged. "But we'll put on your new Christmas sweater to keep you nice and warm."

Of course, Marvin hated wearing sweaters or coats, but it really was too cold to take him outside without one.

"And since you're obviously too tired to keep up your end of this conversation, I guess it's bedtime," Serena said.

Bedtime was another familiar word to him, and Marvin immediately hopped down off the sofa and raced over to the doggy door. But he sat obediently on his mat until she said "okay," then pushed through the flap and went outside to do his business.

A few minutes later, he was back, and immediately went to his bed in the corner.

Serena retreated to her bedroom—where Molly was still curled up in the middle of the mattress.

"You could at least move over and give me some room," she grumbled.

Of course, the cat didn't budge. Not until Serena had fluffed up her pillows and tucked herself in under the covers.

Then Molly crawled up to snuggle against Serena's chest, and purred contentedly.

Serena would never reject the calico's affection, but she couldn't deny that she longed for a different kind of company in her bed. As she drifted off to sleep, she was thinking of Bailey's strong arms around her, his heart beating in sync with her own.

Tuesday morning, Bailey spoke to Dan's wife on the phone. Annie had assured him that her husband was feeling better, but they agreed it wasn't worth the risk of exposing the kids to any remnants of the virus that might be lingering.

He should have dreaded the fact that he had

to don the Santa suit again. Instead, Bailey found himself whistling as he drove to the elementary school, where he'd made arrangements to meet Mrs. Claus in the parking lot.

They walked into the school together and were directed to the teachers' lounge to change into their costumes. He zipped up Serena's dress and tied her apron; she secured his padding and whitened his brows. It was almost like they were a real married couple, helping one another get ready for a social engagement.

Only a few days earlier, he'd been sweaty and nervous and not at all looking forward to stepping out from behind the curtain and facing the group of children waiting in the community center. Today, there was no curtain. Today, they walked through the double doors of the gymnasium, but he felt much more comfortable and relaxed with Serena beside him.

He caught Janie's eye when he entered the gym, and the way her smile widened, she'd obviously recognized Uncle Bailey as the man be-hind Kris Kringle's white beard. But, of course, she didn't reveal his identity to anyone.

When the principal invited him to say a few words, he took advantage of the opportunity to explain that Christmas wasn't just about what they wanted to find under their trees the morn-ing of December 25 but also about giving, and he encouraged them to talk to their parents about supporting Presents for Patriots in any way that they could.

As the afternoon progressed, he thought ev-erything was going well. And then one of the kids—a little girl in second grade with rein-deer antlers mounted onto a headband set in her curly red hair—climbed up onto his lap.

"Ho ho ho," Bailey said. "And what would you like for Christmas?"

Unlike most of the other kids who'd made a request for the usual variety of toys and games, she looked at him with big green eyes filled with worry and sadness and said, "I want my daddy to come home."

Which, of course, wasn't a wish that even the real Santa—if he existed—could grant.

Bailey was at a complete loss because he didn't have any idea where the child's father was or what could be preventing him from being with his family for the holiday. Maybe the little girl's parents were separated or even divorced. Maybe the father was traveling on business or serving overseas in the military. It was even possible that the child's father had passed away, ensuring that her wish was never going to come true.

He glanced, helplessly, hopelessly, at his missus.

And, once again, she came to his rescue and saved the day.

Crouching beside his chair, Serena spoke quietly to the child. "Your daddy's got an important job to do, Harley, and he can't come home until it's done. But I promise that he misses you and your mommy and your brothers as much as you miss him, and I know his wish for you would be that you have happy Christmas memories to share with him when he calls home."

The little girl nodded solemnly, eager to believe every word that Mrs. Claus said to her.

"So is there anything special you'd like to find under the tree on Christmas morning?" Santa asked her again.

This time, she responded without hesitation, confirming that although her first wish was to spend the holiday with her father, she was still a child. "A Stardust Stacie doll would be something good to tell daddy about."

"I'll see what I can do," Santa promised, even as he wondered if the doll would be more readily available than the pocket toys that Serena had told him were so popular this season.

Thankfully, Harley's request was the only snag in Santa's visit to the school. After all the children who wanted to share their wishes with Santa had done so, Mr. and Mrs. Claus retreated to the staff lounge to change out of their costumes and assume their real identities again.

"Who was the little girl who asked about her father coming home for Christmas?" Bailey asked Serena, as he rolled up his enormous red pants.

"Harley Williams," she said. "She's the youngest of three kids. Her mom works at the library and her dad is a marine, currently stationed in Syria."

"Do you know everything about everyone in this town?" he wondered aloud.

"Hardly," she told him. "But the family also has two cats—Bert and Ernie. You'd be amazed how much you learn about people when you help take care of their pets."

"So it would seem," he agreed, stuffing the pants and jacket into the costume bag. "And it seems that I owe you thanks for bailing me out—again."

"It was my pleasure."

"Actually, it was kind of fun today," he acknowledged.

She laughed at the surprise in his voice. "Yes, it was."

He wanted to say something else, something to prolong their conversation and give him an excuse to spend a few more minutes in her company.

It was strange to think that he'd only met her four days earlier, but between the Santa gigs and the Presents for Patriots event and the hot cocoa at Daisy's, they'd spent a lot of time together over those few days. And when he hadn't been with her, he'd been thinking about her.

He suspected that Serena was equally reluctant to part company with him, because after he'd stuffed the costumes in his truck, she asked, "Do you want to go for a ride with me? I'll bring you back here after."

"After what?"

She just smiled, and the sweet curve of her lips was like the sun breaking through the clouds on a gray day.

"Are you game to come with me or not?" she challenged.

Hmm…go back to Sunshine Farm and the chores that were always waiting? Or spend another hour—and maybe more—in the company of a bright and beautiful woman?

It was a no-brainer.

Because the more time he spent with Serena, the more he wanted to be with her. There was something warm and sincere about her that appealed to him. And okay, she was gorgeous and sexy, too, and he was far more attracted to her than he was ready to acknowledge—even to himself.

His romantic history wasn't particularly extensive or successful. Prior to meeting and falling in love with Emily, he'd only dated a few women. Growing up in Rust Creek Falls, he'd spent most of his waking hours at Sunshine Farm, doing any of the endless chores that filled the hours from sunup to sundown. And when those chores were finally done, he was usually too exhausted to go out and do anything else.

The one night he'd let Luke convince him that they deserved to have some fun had ended up being the worst night of his life.

He shook off the weight of those memories and focused his attention on the present—and the woman presently waiting for a response to her question.

"Why don't I drive and bring you back to your vehicle after?" he suggested. Because yeah, he was one of those guys who liked to be in the driver's seat—both literally and figuratively.

"After what?" she teasingly echoed his question.

He shrugged.

"And that's why I'm driving," she said. "Because I know where we're going." She thumbed the button on her key fob to unlock the doors.

He went to the driver's side first. She pulled back the hand that held her keys, as if she expected him to try to take them from her, but he only opened the door for her.

"Thank you," she said, appreciative of the gesture.

"You're welcome," he said, waiting until she'd slid into the driver's seat to close the door for her.

After he was buckled in, she turned her vehicle toward the highway, heading out of town.

After only a few minutes, Bailey figured out that they were making their way toward Falls Mountain and the actual Rust Creek Falls that gave the town its name. They passed a picnic area and signs that guided visitors to a viewing area for the falls. She continued to drive farther up the mountain, finally turning off the main road to park in a small gravel lot at the base of the trail that led to Owl Rock—the lookout point named for the large white boulder that resembled the bird and protruded out over the falls, as if keeping watch over them.

During the spring and summer months, vehicles would be packed closely together and the trails would be busy with hikers and families. But it was early December and too cold for most people, aside from the most hardy outdoor enthusiasts. Apparently Serena was one of those enthusiasts.

"Nice day for a hike," he commented, as he followed her up the trail.

And it was, because although the air was frigid, the sun was shining. Also, he had a spectacular view of her shapely butt, encased in snug-fitting denim.

"I haven't been up here since I was a teenager," he told her, as they arrived at the lookout point. "In fact, I'd almost forgotten this place existed."

"It's one of my favorite places in Rust Creek Falls," she confided, sitting down on a flat outcropping of rock with her legs crossed beneath her. "My grandmother brought me here when I first came to Rust Creek Falls, and whenever I'm feeling down, I find myself drawn back. Being close to nature always lifts my spirits."

"Why did you want to come here today?" he asked her.

She was silent for a minute before responding. "Because Harley's request about her dad brought back some painful memories."

As a man who carefully guarded his own secrets, he was reluctant to pry into hers. On the other hand, she'd invited him to come here with her today, which suggested that she wanted someone to talk to.

He lowered himself onto the rock beside her,

sitting close enough that their shoulders were touching. "What kind of memories?"

"When I was just about Harley's age, I went to see Santa and asked him to bring my sister home from the hospital in time for Christmas."

"I didn't know you had a sister," Bailey admitted, surprised by her revelation.

"I don't." She unfolded her legs and drew her knees up to her chest, wrapping her arms around them. "Not anymore."

He didn't prompt her for more information. She would tell him more when she was ready.

"I was an only child for the first six years of my life," she began. "An only child who *begged* for a brother or sister. And when my parents finally told me that there was a baby in my mommy's tummy, I couldn't wait for her to be born.

"I don't know if my parents knew for sure that they were having a girl, but I always thought of her as my sister. It was probably wishful thinking on my part, because I was seven, and I thought boys were mostly gross and dumb and I really wanted a sister."

She paused for a minute, gathering her thoughts—or maybe her composure.

"Then something went wrong, and my mom had to go into the hospital early. It must have been just before Halloween, because I was sucking on a lollipop that I'd stolen out of the bucket of candy my mom had bought for trick-or-treaters when Grams came into my room and told me that she was going to be staying with us for a few days.

"Miriam was born six weeks before her due date. I remember asking my grandmother why she didn't seem happy when she told me the news. She said it was because the baby was too small and that she might not make it.

"I didn't understand what she meant. The only information that registered with me was that I finally had a sister.

"So my grandmother bluntly told me that Miriam might die. I refused to believe it. Babies didn't die. Old people died. And I demanded to meet my sister.

"A few days later, Grams finally gave in and took me up to the hospital to see my parents and the baby. Miriam was in an incubator, though of course I didn't know what it was at the time. I only knew that she had tubes stuck in various parts of her body and she didn't look anything like a baby—at least nothing like Mr. and Mrs. Wakefield's baby, the focus of everyone's attention and well wishes at church earlier that morning.

"I think I started to cry, because my dad picked me up and tried to soothe me. And my mom got mad at Grams for bringing me to the hospital, but she argued that it was important for me to see my sister, in case anything happened.

"This made my mom cry and my dad told her

to go. But I got to stay for a while, snuggling with my mom while my dad told us that everything was going to be fine, because Mimi— that's what we called her—was strong, just like me. And he promised that we'd all be celebrating Christmas together in a few weeks.

"And he was right, although it wasn't really as simple or easy as that. Mimi had to stay in the hospital until she was a lot bigger and stronger, and the doctors warned that could take several weeks or even months.

"One night, in mid-December, my dad said that he had a surprise. Instead of going to the hospital, he took me to the local mall to see Santa." Serena nudged Bailey playfully with her shoulder. "Back then, it was what you did to see the big guy, because we didn't have a community center in town or any handsome cowboys willing to put on a padded red suit."

Taking his cue from her deliberate attempt

to lighten the mood, Bailey lifted his brows. "You think I'm handsome?"

"To quote Ellie Traub, 'all those Stockton boys are handsome devils.'"

"Good to know," he said, equal parts flattered and embarrassed by the older woman's assessment. "But you were telling me about your visit to Santa."

"Right," she agreed. "My dad took me to see Santa and I thought of all the wishes I'd carefully printed on my Christmas list to decide which one I wanted most of all. That year, it was a toss-up between Mouse Trap, the board game, and a new pair of ballet slippers. But when it was finally my turn, all I could think was that I wanted my baby sister to come home from the hospital for Christmas."

"Did Santa deliver?" he asked gently.

She nodded. "Mimi came home the afternoon of December 24. It was as if we got our very own Christmas miracle. The next morning,

I didn't even race downstairs to see if Santa had left any presents under the tree. Instead, I rushed across the hall to the nursery, to make sure she was still there.

"And she was. The Mouse Trap game and ballet slippers that I unwrapped later were bonuses—all I really wanted was my sister. Of course, she needed a lot of attention," Serena continued. "And I was happy to give it to her. Happy to finally have the sister I'd always wanted.

"If she cried, I wanted to be the one to pick her up. If she was hungry, I wanted to give her a bottle. Even when she was content to sit in her high chair or play swing, I was there, reading to her or singing the songs I'd learned at school. Long before she could talk, she would clap her hands and kick her feet whenever she listened to music."

She smiled at the memory. "And Christmas carols were her favorite. Maybe not that first

Christmas," she acknowledged. "That year she mostly seemed fascinated by the colored lights and sparkly ornaments on the tree. But by the following year, when she was thirteen months old, she was munching on sugar cookies and tearing the bows and paper off presents. The year after that, she shook colored sugar onto the cookies before she ate them and even helped hang some sparkly ornaments on the tree."

Serena dropped her chin to her bent knees, her gaze focused on something in the distance—or maybe something in the past. "And then, just a few weeks after her third birthday, she disappeared."

Chapter Six

*D*isappeared?

Just when Bailey started to think he knew where the story was leading, it took a major detour. He caught the sheen of moisture in Serena's eyes, noted the tension in the arms that hugged her legs tight. He shifted on the rock so that he was sitting behind her, his legs splayed to bracket her hips, his arms wrapped around her.

"My parents had planned a special trip for all of us," she continued. "We went to Missoula to participate in the Parade of Lights and enjoy a performance of *The Nutcracker*. Of course, Mimi was too young to understand the show and she fidgeted through the whole thing, but I'd been dancing for five years by then, and I was completely entranced. Next to Mimi, that was the best Christmas present I'd ever received.

"The morning of our planned return to Rust Creek Falls, we stopped at the Holiday Made Fair so that my parents could do some last-minute shopping. It was crowded with booths and toys and goodies and lots of people. I was under strict instructions to hold tight to Mimi's hand, and I did." She swallowed. "Until I didn't."

He hugged her a little tighter, a wordless offer of comfort and encouragement.

"She saw the doll first," Serena said, resuming her narrative. "It was a replica of the Sugar Plum Fairy and she pulled me to it. There was a whole bin of them, and Mimi tugged her hand from mine so that she could pick one up. And I picked up another one, admiring the intricate details of her costume, and I turned to show Mimi something, but she wasn't there anymore.

"It happened that fast," she said, her voice hollow. "She was right beside me...and then she was gone. My parents were, of course, frantic. We didn't celebrate the holidays—we were too busy looking for Mimi. But she'd disappeared without a trace. The police got all kinds of tips and followed countless leads, but nothing ever panned out. As days turned into weeks and weeks into months, we began to lose hope that she would ever come home again.

"I know she's out there somewhere," Serena insisted. "And I believe with my whole heart that she's alive...just lost to us.

"By the summer, my mother was self-medicating with alcohol. I didn't know what that meant, except that I heard my dad say it to my grandmother. I did know that my mom stumbled around a lot, ran her words together so that sometimes I couldn't understand what she was saying, and slept a lot. And, of course, my parents fought. All the time. Several months later, before Christmas the following year, my dad took off."

And only a few days earlier, Bailey had accused Serena of not understanding that happiness was a fickle emotion that could be snatched away without warning. No wonder she'd cautioned him about making assumptions, because she did understand. Because she'd experienced a loss as profound as his own.

"He left a note," she continued. "It wasn't like when Mimi disappeared. But the note didn't say much more than that he felt as if he'd failed his family, and every day with us—without Mimi—was a reminder of that."

"I'm so sorry, Serena." The words sounded

so meaningless, even to his own ears, but they were all he had to offer.

"There wasn't anything joyful about Christmas that year, either," she said.

"I can only imagine how difficult it would be to celebrate anything after losing a child," he acknowledged.

"Mimi's disappearance was devastating for all of us," Serena agreed. "But my parents had two children—and they didn't lose both of them."

But Serena had effectively lost both of her parents after the disappearance of her sister. And Bailey suspected that she'd been deeply scarred by it.

"Of course, my mom's drinking got even worse after my dad left. And Child Protective Services got involved in the New Year after my teacher called to report that I frequently wore the same clothes to school several days in a row and sometimes didn't have any food in my lunch box.

"That's when my grandmother came to stay with us again. She tried to get my mother back on track—and Amanda tried to stop drinking. But inevitably, after a few weeks—or sometimes not more than a few days—she'd decide that she needed 'just one drink' to take the edge off her pain and emptiness. Of course, one drink always turned into two and then three, until eventually she'd end up passed out on the sofa."

Bailey had been there—alone in that dark place where it seemed that nothing could take the edge off his aching emptiness and the only recourse was to drown his sorrows. He didn't do that anymore, but he could appreciate that it was a slippery slope and he was grateful that he'd managed to find his footing before he'd slipped too far.

"After a few such incidents, my grandmother

talked her into going to rehab. She completed a thirty-day inpatient program and, when she came home, assured us that she'd turned a corner. A few days later, on what would have been her thirteenth wedding anniversary, she got drunk again."

"Significant dates and special occasions are triggers for a lot of people," he observed.

Serena nodded. "But as much as my grandmother was worried about her daughter's downward spiral, she was even more worried about me. So she packed up all my stuff and brought me to Rust Creek Falls to live with her. And she told my mother that, when she was ready to prove that her daughter was more important than the contents of a bottle, she would be welcome to stay with her, too."

"Sounds like a strong dose of tough love," Bailey remarked.

"It was tough on Grams, too. She wanted to make everything right, but she couldn't fight

Amanda's addiction. So she focused her attention and efforts on me. I had sporadic contact with Amanda over the next few years," she confided. "I still feel guilty saying this out loud, but those were some of the most normal—and best—years of my childhood. Maybe it was a little strange that I lived with my grandmother rather than my mother or father, but I had no cause for complaint. I had regular meals and clean clothes, willing help with homework and even a chaperone for occasional school trips."

"I'm glad you had her," Bailey said.

"I was lucky," Serena acknowledged.

He hadn't had the same fortune when he lost his parents. In fact, Matthew and Agnes Baldwin had essentially told their three oldest grandsons to fend for themselves—and allowed their two youngest granddaughters to be adopted, forcing the split of seven children grieving the deaths of their parents.

"Does your grandmother still live in Rust Creek Falls?" he asked Serena now.

She shook her head. "A few years ago, after I'd graduated from college and she was sure my mother's life was back on track, she decided her old bones couldn't handle the cold any longer, and she moved to Arizona." She smiled a little. "It's been good for her. She's taken up golf, plays bridge and does water aerobics—and she's got a new beau."

"You can be happy for her and still miss her," Bailey assured her.

"I do miss her," she admitted. "But I've also realized that I maybe relied on her too much. I don't think the warmer climate was her only reason for leaving Rust Creek Falls. I think she wanted me to stand on my own two feet—not to see *if* I could, but to show me *that* I could. Because she always had a lot more confidence in me than I had in myself."

"I'd say her faith was well-founded."

"My grandmother's a wise woman," she acknowledged. "She's the one who taught me to focus on my happy memories of the holidays."

"That couldn't have been easy," he noted. In fact, considering how much heartache she'd endured—and so much of it focused around this time of year—he might have found the task impossible.

"It took me a while to look past all the bad stuff and remember the good stuff," she confided to him. "Although we only celebrated three Christmases together with Mimi, those were the happiest Christmases of my life. Every memory of my sister is a happy memory, and she loved everything about Christmas."

"You're an amazing woman, Serena Langley."

"I'm not sure about that," she said. "But focusing on the happy memories is the one thing—the only thing—I can do that helps me get through. And in remembering Mimi's holiday joy, I've rediscovered my own."

Her outgoing and optimistic demeanor had led him to make certain assumptions about her, but those assumptions couldn't have been more wrong. Not knowing what to say to her now, certain there were no words to express his regrets and sympathy, he merely pulled her closer.

Serena dropped her head back against his shoulder, and when her lips curved a little as she looked up at him, he knew that he was forgiven for what he'd said the other day.

And then his head tipped forward…and his lips brushed against hers.

He hadn't consciously decided to kiss her. Sure, he'd given the idea more than a passing thought. And yeah, he'd wondered if her lips would be as soft as they looked or taste as sweet as he imagined. And maybe, when they'd been dancing at the Presents for Patriots fund-raiser, he'd considered breaching the scant distance that separated their mouths.

But he'd resisted the impulse, because he knew that kissing her was a bad idea for a lot of reasons. First, after the breakdown of his marriage, he was wary of any kind of romantic involvement. Second, even if he was looking to get involved, it would be a mistake to hook up with a woman who was both a colleague and friend of his sister-in-law. Third—

He abandoned his mental list in favor of focusing on the moment—and the fact that Serena was kissing him back. And her lips were as soft as they looked, and their taste was even sweeter than he'd imagined.

And he realized that sitting on Owl Rock and kissing Serena was the absolute highlight of his day. His week. His month. Possibly even his whole year.

He lifted a hand to cup the back of her head, his fingers diving through silky strands of hair, tilting her head so that he could deepen the kiss. She didn't protest when his tongue slid between her lips but met it with her own.

He wrapped his other arm around her middle and dragged her onto his lap. Her arms lifted to his shoulders. Her legs wrapped around his waist. He wanted to touch her; he wanted his hands on her bare skin. But they were outside in Montana in December, which meant there were at least a half dozen layers of clothing and outerwear between them.

After a while—two minutes? Ten? He didn't know, he'd lost all track of time while he was kissing her—she drew her mouth away from his.

"Maybe we should…slow things down," she suggested a little breathlessly.

He took a moment to draw the sharp cold air into his own lungs. "That would probably be the smart thing to do," he agreed. "But it's not what I want to do."

"Right now, it's not what I want, either," she admitted. "But I haven't had much success with romantic relationships and I don't want to jeopardize our fledgling friendship by trying to turn it into something more."

"I suck at relationships, too," he told her. "I'm not sure I'm much better at friendships."

"You seem to be doing okay so far."

He appreciated the vote of confidence, but he remained dubious. "You think we're friends?"

"I think we could be," she said.

"Hmm," he said, considering.

"Unless you have so many friends that you don't want another one?"

He chuckled softly. "Before I came back to Rust Creek Falls last year, I'd been gone for a dozen years and lost touch with not just my family but my friends."

"It was after your parents were killed that you left town, wasn't it?"

The surprise he felt must have been reflected

in his expression, because she explained, "I've worked with Annie for almost three years, and when Dan came back—just a few months before you did—it sent her whole life into a tailspin. And sometimes, if we were on break together, she'd talk to me about it."

"So how much of the story do you know?" he wondered.

"I don't know all the details—and most of those that I do know are from her perspective. Essentially that you, Luke and Dan were of legal age, and your grandparents decided that you were able to take care of yourselves so they didn't have to."

He nodded. "That about sums it up," he agreed. "What really sucks is that we all assumed that Sunshine Farm would be lost. Our parents struggled for a lot of years and without my dad around to run the ranch, we couldn't imagine making a go of it. If we'd known that the mortgage was insured, we might have stayed." Then he shook his head. "Who am I kidding? We wouldn't have stayed. We couldn't have. Not after that night."

That night was the night both of his parents had been killed by a drunk driver. And the events of that night continued to haunt him and would undoubtedly do so forever.

"Look," Serena said, holding out a hand to catch a delicate flake on her palm. "It's snowing."

"So it is," he agreed, noting the fluffy flakes falling from the sky. "It's also getting colder by the minute."

"I know. I can't feel my butt anymore."

"I could feel it for you," he suggested, in an obvious effort to lighten the mood.

"I appreciate the offer, but maybe another time," she said, as she untangled her legs and rose to her feet. "We should be heading back now, anyway."

"You're probably right," he agreed, understanding only too well that driving conditions on the mountain roads could turn hazardous quickly.

But as they turned back toward the trail, he asked, "Did Owl Rock work its magic for you today?"

She nodded. "It's always so peaceful up here. But even better today was having someone to talk to."

"Glad to be of service," he told her.

At the top of the narrow trail, Bailey insisted on taking the lead so that he could check for slippery patches on the descent. But he also took her hand, to ensure she didn't fall behind.

The weather in Montana wasn't just unpredictable, it could change fast—and had done so while they were up at Owl Rock. By the time they got back to her vehicle, she had to pull her snow brush out to clear off her windows.

"You get in," Bailey instructed. "I'll take care of this."

She didn't object to that but handed him the brush and slid in behind the wheel, turning on the engine and cranking up the heat.

A few minutes later, Bailey put the brush away and took his seat on the passenger side.

"I'm happy to drive, if you want," he told her.

Her only response was to shift into Drive and pull out of the gravel lot.

At the midway point of their return journey, Bailey said, "Since we almost go right past Wings To Go on our way back to the school, why don't we stop in there to grab some dinner?"

"I can't," Serena said regretfully. "I've got animals waiting to be fed at home."

"Do you have dinner waiting, too?"

She shook her head. "I wasn't thinking that far ahead when I left home this morning."

"Do you like wings?"

"Who doesn't?"

"Well, here's an interesting fact about Wings

To Go," he said. "Customers can actually place an order…and then take it away from the restaurant."

"No kidding," she said, sounding bemused. "I'll bet that's what the To Go part of the name refers to."

"And with that in mind, here's plan B," he said. "After you take me back to my truck and go home to feed your animals, I'll pick up wings and bring them over to feed us. What do you think of that plan?"

"I think I like that plan," she agreed. "Especially if it includes honey-barbecue wings."

After dropping Bailey off at his truck in the elementary school parking lot, Serena hurried home. Not just because she knew Marvin, Molly and Max would be waiting for her, but because she wanted to tidy up a little before Bailey showed up. She didn't think her apartment was a mess, but earlier in the day she'd been so focused on the anticipation of seeing Bailey that she honestly couldn't remember if she'd left her lunch dishes in the sink or her pajamas on the floor in the bathroom.

As she raced around the apartment, tidying a stack of mail on the counter, wiping crumbs— and a smudge of something sticky—off the table and pushing the Swiffer around, Marvin chased after her, delighted with what he assumed was a new game.

"It's not a game, it's housework," she told him. "And I do this at least once a week."

But she didn't usually clean at such a frantic pace, and Marvin refused to believe she wasn't playing with him.

She gave him his dinner, hoping the food would take his attention away from the Swiffer. The diversion worked—for the whole two minutes that it took him to empty his bowl. But she finished putting her apartment in order—and even managed to run a brush through her hair and dab on some lip gloss before she saw Bailey's truck pull into one of the designated visitor parking spots at the back of the building.

Marvin raced toward the door a full half minute before the bell rang, having been alerted to the presence of a visitor by the sound of feet climbing the stairs. Though he could easily have gone through the doggy door to greet the newcomer, Serena had been strict in his training to ensure his safety and that of her guests. So now he waited in eager anticipation, his entire back end wagging.

"No jumping," she admonished firmly as she opened the door.

Bailey's eyes skimmed over her, a slow perusal from the top of her head to the thick wool socks on her feet. "I wasn't planning on jumping," he drawled. "But I can't deny that the idea is intriguing."

"Ha ha," she said, taking the bag from his hands so that he could remove his boots.

As he reached down to unfasten the laces, Marvin whimpered.

"You must be Marvin," Bailey said, and offered his hand for the dog to sniff.

Marvin sniffed, then licked, then shoved his snout into the visitor's palm. Bailey chuckled and scratched the dog's chin.

Serena set plates and napkins on the table. "What can I get you to drink? I've got cola, root beer, real beer, milk or water."

"Cola sounds good," he said.

"Glass or can?"

"Can works."

She retrieved two cans from the fridge and set them on the table, then glanced back at the entranceway to discover that Bailey was sitting on the tile floor with Marvin sprawled across his lap. The dog's belly was exposed and his tongue lolled out of his mouth as his new best friend gave him a vigorous belly rub.

She shook her head. "Such an attention whore."

"I am not," Bailey denied.

"I was referring to the dog."

"Oh." He gave Marvin a couple more rubs, then carefully heaved the dog off his lap and stood up. He made his way into the kitchen and washed his hands at the sink. Marvin kept pace with him, practically glued to his shin.

"I'm the one who feeds you," Serena felt compelled to remind her canine companion.

Marvin wagged his whole body, but he didn't move away from Bailey.

And when Bailey took a seat at the table, Marvin settled at his feet.

"I feel like I talked your ear off when we were up at Owl Rock today," Serena said as she used the tongs to transfer several wings from the box to her plate. "But the truth is, I don't often talk about my sister or her disappearance. In fact, I doubt if more than a handful of people in this town even know what happened before I came to live with my grandmother all those years ago."

"Your secrets are safe with me," he promised.

"I'm not worried," she said. "But I'm thinking that it's your turn to tell me your life story."

"There's not much to tell." He took the tongs she offered, then proceeded to pick out half a dozen wings. "And you already know the highlights."

"I know why you went away, but I don't know anything about where you went or what you did when you left Rust Creek Falls."

"Me, Luke and Danny headed to Wyoming together and found work on a big spread in Cheyenne. We stayed there for about six months together before we parted ways."

"Why?" she wondered aloud.

He shrugged. "Maybe because we had different goals and ambitions. Or maybe because we shared the same guilt and regrets."

She picked a piece of meat off the bone. "Where did you go after Cheyenne?"

"Jackson Hole for a while, then Newcastle and Douglas."

"So you stayed in Wyoming?"

"For a few years," he acknowledged. "Then I made my way to New Mexico."

"That was quite a move," she remarked.

He licked honey-barbecue sauce off his thumb. "There was a girl," he admitted.

"Ahh, I should have guessed."

He shook his head. "I promise you, I'm not in the habit of chasing women halfway across the country. That was the first—and absolute last—time."

"Putting aside the fact that New Mexico isn't really across the county but directly south of Wyoming, she must have been someone really special."

"Actually, she was my wife."

Chapter Seven

Wife?

Serena nearly choked on a mouthful of cola.

Bailey watched her cough and sputter, his brow furrowed with concern. "Are you okay?"

"Yeah." She coughed again. "I'm fine." She took a careful sip of her soda. "I didn't realize you'd been married."

"Only because I was young and foolish enough to believe that love conquers all."

"I'm sorry it didn't work out," she said. "But

at least you were willing to take a chance on love."

"I was young and foolish," he said again.

"And now you're old and wise?" she teased.

"Older and wiser, anyway. No way am I ever going to make that mistake again."

"You don't believe in love anymore?"

"I don't know," he said. "I mean, each of my brothers and even my sister Bella seems to have found a forever match, so maybe it's just me. Maybe I'm not capable of loving somebody that way."

"You must have loved your wife."

"I thought I did," he acknowledged. "But in the end, whatever I felt for her wasn't enough."

"It takes two people to make a relationship work," she pointed out. "Or allow it to fail."

"So it would seem," he agreed.

"Then again—" she picked up another wing "—what do I know?"

"You've never been in love?"

She shook her head. "The longest relationship I've ever had is with Molly."

His brows lifted. "Molly?"

"My cat," she reminded him.

"That's right. You've got Marvin, Molly and…"

"Max," she supplied.

"So where are Molly and Max?"

"Hiding," she admitted. "They're both leery of strangers. And—" she glanced at the bulldog under the table "—*not* attention whores."

"Why all the animals?" he wondered aloud.

She shrugged. "I've always loved animals."

"That would explain why you became a vet tech," he commented. "Not why you've turned your home into a mini animal shelter."

"And…they love me back. Unconditionally."

"That's something a lot of human beings have a problem with," he said.

"Yeah. Sometimes even the ones who are supposed to love you."

"Like your dad," he guessed. "And my grand-parents."

She nodded. "All my animals want from me is a roof over their heads, food in their bowls, some interaction and playtime, and the occasional lazy Sunday morning snuggle in bed."

"They sleep with you?"

"No. They have their own beds, but some-times, if I'm feeling lazy and slip back between the covers after feeding them their breakfast, they'll follow me into the bedroom and want to cuddle with me."

"Even the cat?"

She nodded. "Molly is a surprisingly affec-tionate feline at times—at least with me," she clarified. "And Max. She absolutely adores the bunny. She's less fond of strangers."

"Marvin doesn't consider me a stranger," he noted.

"Marvin is forever devoted to anyone who gives him an ear scratch or belly rub. Or *t-r-e-a-t-s*," she said, purposely spelling the word so that the dog wouldn't get excited about the possibility of getting one. "Which reminds me—I guess my bid didn't win the Canine Christmas basket at the silent auction?"

Bailey shook his head. "You were outbid by Lissa Christensen."

"That's good for Presents for Patriots, but sad for Marvin," she said.

"And then Lissa Christensen was outbid by me."

"*You* bought the basket?"

He nodded.

"Why?"

"Because I know how much you wanted it," he said.

"You bought it for me?"

"Well, for Marvin, actually."

"That was really sweet," she said, then laughed when he winced. "How much do I owe you? I don't know how much cash I have, but I could write you a check."

"You're not writing me a check," he protested.

"Worried it might bounce?"

He shook his head. "I mean you're not paying for the basket."

"But you bought it for my dog."

"That's right," he said. "*I* bought it for you to give to him."

"Then I'll say thank you, and check Marvin's name off my shopping list."

"Yeah, I guess I should probably get started on mine," he acknowledged.

"You haven't even started your shopping yet?"

"It's only December 4," he pointed out.

"No," she denied. "It's *already* December 4."

"To-may-to, to-mah-to," he said.

"You'll be saying something different when you're fighting the frantic and desperate masses of last-minute shoppers at the mall on Christmas Eve."

"I won't wait until Christmas Eve. Probably."

She shook her head despairingly. "I'm planning to go into Kalispell to do some shopping on Saturday," she told him. "You're welcome to come with me, if you want."

"I guess it wouldn't hurt to get a head start this year."

"You'll be one of the early birds," she said dryly.

Bailey just grinned. Then he said, "Seriously though, I appreciate your offer to let me tag along."

"It's not a problem," she assured him. "But you're not allowed to complain if we're gone most of the day."

"I can't make any promises there," he said.

"Then I can't promise that you'll get a ride back home again."

When all the wing bones had been picked clean and the dishes cleared away, Bailey thanked Serena for her hospitality and made his way to the door.

He could have come up with an excuse to linger; he could have requested a cup of coffee before he hit the road or offered to take Marvin for a walk or asked her to turn on the TV to check the score of the game—because there was always a game of some sort playing—and then allowed himself to get caught up in the action on the screen for a while. But when he realized that he was searching for a reason to stay, he knew it was time to go. Because the more time he spent with Serena, the more he wanted to be with her, and that was a dangerous desire.

Besides, he was going to see her again on Saturday.

Yeah, Saturday was four days away, but maybe a little space and time was what he needed to give himself some perspective and remember that he wasn't going to get involved.

Not with Serena. Not with anyone. Not ever again.

But when she walked him to the door, he was more than a little tempted to kiss her goodbye.

But she'd asked him to slow things down. She wanted to be *friends*. He had his doubts about that possibility—mostly because he really wanted to get her naked, and in his experience, lust tended to get in the way of friendship—but he decided to try it her way for a while.

So he didn't kiss her goodbye, but the memory of the kiss they'd shared at Owl Rock teased his mind and heated his body as he climbed into his cold truck and drove away.

But before he could head back to Sunshine Farm, he had one more stop to make. He'd promised to return the costumes to Annie after the visit to the elementary school—a promise he'd nearly forgotten until he spotted the bulky bags in the back seat.

"There he is," Annie said when she responded to his knock on the door.

"Who is it?" Janie asked from somewhere inside the house.

"Uncle Grooge," her mother responded.

"Bah, humbug," Bailey said, playing along as he held out the costume bags, and heard Janie giggle.

"Hmm…" Annie took the bags and stepped away from the door so he could enter. "That doesn't sound quite as cynical as it did a few days ago. Maybe this suit has magic powers."

He ignored her comment to focus on his niece, seated at the table with her schoolbooks open in front of her. "Homework?" he guessed.

She nodded. "Science," she said, her expression and her tone reflecting displeasure. "Dad was helping me, but Mom ordered him to go rest when you showed up."

"I ordered him to rest because he's still recuperating," Annie said in a no-nonsense mom voice.

"Oh, right."

The exchange struck Bailey as a little odd, but his sister-in-law didn't pause long enough for him to ponder it.

"Considering that school let out almost five hours ago, I hope you're not just getting back from the Santa gig now," she remarked.

"Of course not. Me and Serena went for a drive afterward," he admitted. "And then we decided to get some dinner."

"Like a date?" Janie asked.

"No," he immediately replied.

"Sounds like a date to me," his niece insisted.

"What do you know about dating?" he asked her.

"Nothing," she said with a sigh. "Nothing at all."

"Homework," Annie said, in an effort to redirect her daughter's attention. Then to Bailey, "But your non-date with Serena is interesting."

"What's so interesting about it?" he challenged.

"Just that, as far as I know, you haven't dated anyone since you came back to Rust Creek Falls."

"And I'm not dating anyone now," he said firmly.

His sister-in-law sighed. "Well, thank you again for filling in for your brother today."

"How's he doing?"

"Much better. In fact, he's in the living room watching TV if you want to say hi."

So Bailey went through to the living room, where his brother was stretched out on the sofa. Shifting his gaze to the screen, he saw that, sure enough, there was a game on.

"Hey," Dan said, clicking the mute button on the remote. "How'd it go today?"

"Pretty good," Bailey allowed.

"Janie said you were a very believable Santa Claus."

"Ho ho ho," he said, affecting the persona.

Dan nodded. "Not bad for a Grooge."

Bailey just shook his head.

"Seriously though, I appreciate you filling in for me again," his brother said.

"It wasn't really that big a deal," Bailey said.

"It was to me. For too many years, when I was living on my own, I forgot what it meant to be part of a family, to know there were people I could count on to help me out."

"I'm sorry I bailed on you all those years ago."

Dan shook his head. "That's not what I'm saying."

"I'm sorry anyway."

"We all made mistakes. And it really did mean the world to me that you found your way back to Rust Creek Falls for my wedding."

"That was just unfortunate timing on my part," Bailey said, not entirely joking.

"So you've said—on more than one occasion," his brother acknowledged dryly.

"But you and Annie…you really do work," he said. "Not just as a couple but a family."

"Coming home was the best thing I ever did," Dan said. "I only wish I'd found the courage to do so a lot sooner—then maybe I wouldn't have missed the first eleven years of Janie's life."

Yeah, it sucked that his brother had lost so much time with his daughter. And though Bailey didn't doubt that they'd hit some rough spots as they got to know one another, they were growing closer every day.

If Dan held on to any resentment because his daughter also continued to be close to Hank Harlow, who'd raised her as his own for the first decade of her life—even after divorcing Annie—he was smart enough not to show it. And if Bailey could believe his brother, Dan was sincerely grateful that Hank had been there for Janie during those years that her biological father wasn't.

"I'm hoping that it won't take too much longer for you to figure out that coming home was the best thing you ever did, too," Dan said.

Bailey shrugged, deliberately noncommittal.

When he'd shown up in Rust Creek Falls the previous December, he'd had no intention of staying for any length of time. He only wanted to touch base with his siblings before he moved on again. Almost twelve months later, he was still in town, still trying to figure out a plan for his own life.

He should be on his way, but things felt... unfinished. Though he'd reconnected with all of his brothers and two of his sisters, he knew that there would be a void in all their lives until Liza was found.

Bella's husband, Hudson Jones, had willingly bankrolled the search for his wife's missing siblings. Of course, Hudson had all kinds of money to throw around and there was no doubt the multimillionaire would do anything for Bella. In fact, it was the bigshot PI he'd hired—David Bradford—who'd managed to track down their brother Luke in Cheyenne, notwithstanding the fact that a payroll glitch had caused him to be working under the name Lee Stanton at the time.

Bailey had come back to Rust Creek Falls of his own volition a few weeks after Luke. But while the PI continued to look for their youngest sister, he'd yet to make any significant progress in that search.

"Anyway," Bailey said, not wanting to dwell on past mistakes or current problems, "I'm glad you've finally kicked back at that virus or flu or whatever knocked you down."

"Not as glad as I am," Dan said. "I don't mind staying in bed all day if my beautiful wife is there with me, but fever and chills sure can put a damper on a man's enjoyment between the sheets."

Bailey held up a hand. "I really don't want to hear about your bedroom activities."

"You're just jealous that I have a love life," Dan teased.

Maybe he was envious—not so much of his brother's bedroom activities, but the obvious and deep connection he shared with both his wife and newfound daughter. Dan was part of a family again, and thriving in the roles of husband and father.

Dan and Annie had fallen in love when they were teenagers, and somehow their love had survived not only a dozen years apart but Annie's marriage to another man during that time. Bailey knew there had been issues for them to work through when Dan finally returned to Rust Creek Falls—and a lot of hurts to be forgiven—and he wondered what it would be like to share that kind of relationship with someone.

Bailey had thought he was in love with Emily and wanted to build a life with her, but it quickly became apparent that he and his wife had very different ideas for their future together. He'd taken a chance and he'd blown it. He had no desire to open up his heart and let it be kicked around again.

But even as he reminded himself of that fact, he found his thoughts drifting again, and an image of Serena formed in his mind, tugged at his heart. She was obviously a lot stronger and braver than he was. She'd suffered the loss of her sister and subsequent breakup of her family, and somehow she still managed to greet each day with a smile on her face. Not only that, but she actually looked forward to celebrating the Christmas season and sharing her joy with others—including him.

"So you didn't mind partnering with Serena Langley?" Dan asked, breaking into Bailey's thoughts.

"No, it was fine," he said cautiously.

"Just fine?"

"What do you want me to say?"

His brother shrugged. "I just wondered what's going on with the two of you."

"*You* wondered what's going on?"

"Okay, Annie was wondering," Dan admitted. "You know she and Serena are friends as well as coworkers."

"I do know," Bailey confirmed. "And if your wife wants to know what's going on, maybe she should ask her friend and coworker."

"Believe me, I wouldn't be hassling you if Annie had had any success with her inquiries."

"Maybe Serena hasn't told her anything because there's nothing to tell," Bailey suggested.

"Luke said you danced with her at the fundraiser—and that sparks were flying."

"Maybe between him and Eva," he countered. "But it's nice to know that my brothers have nothing better to do than gossip about me."

"Since you don't tell us anything, it's the only way we can keep up with what's going on in your life."

He wanted to protest that there was nothing to share, but then he remembered the kiss. That kiss had definitely been something, and it made him want more. A lot more.

But that wasn't something he had any intention of sharing with his brother for Dan to then share with the rest of the family.

Even if it was kind of nice to be reunited with his siblings and to know that they cared.

Serena was waiting for Bailey to pick her up for their shopping trip Saturday morning when her phone rang. She intended to let the call go to voice mail, but a quick glance at the display identified the caller as Janet Carswell, causing her to snatch up the receiver.

"Hi, Grams."

"I got your Christmas card in the mail yesterday," her grandmother said. "The pretty winter scene on the front didn't make me miss the snow, but I do miss you."

"I miss you, too," Serena told her.

"How is everything in Rust Creek Falls?"

"Cold and snowy," she said.

"Nothing new?" her grandmother prompted.

"Well, I saw my mom last week."

"How is she?" Grams asked cautiously.

"Good," Serena said, and proceeded to fill her grandmother in on the conversation she'd had with her mother—and on Amanda's new boyfriend.

"I'm glad to hear that my daughter's doing well," Grams said. "But I really want to know what's been going on with my granddaughter and her new man."

"You've been talking to Melba Strickland," she guessed.

"Well, someone needs to keep me up to date with the happenings in Rust Creek Falls."

"I talk to you every week," Serena reminded her grandmother.

"But you always censor the good stuff."

She chuckled. "You only think I do. The truth is, there isn't any good stuff to censor."

"Maybe that's why I worry about you, Rena."

"You don't need to worry about me—I'm doing just fine," she assured her.

"You're alone," Grams said in a gentle tone.

"Hardly."

"Your pets don't count."

"Don't tell them that," Serena cautioned.

Grams sighed. "You've got so much love to give, but you're afraid to give it."

"I'm not afraid."

"It's understandable." Her grandmother forged ahead as if Serena hadn't spoken. "You've been hurt, and deeply, by so many people who were supposed to love you."

"You're the one who always said that whatever doesn't kill us makes us stronger."

"I was paraphrasing Nietzsche," Grams confessed.

"Still, I think there's a lot of truth in that statement."

"And I think you're one of the strongest women I know," her grandmother said. "With one of the softest hearts. But you don't let many people into your heart."

"I let plenty of people into my heart."

"You know what I mean," Grams chided. "You've hardly dated anyone since you broke up with Bobby Ray."

It was true. It was also true that she never should have let herself fall for a man who everyone knew was still carrying a torch for his high school girlfriend—notwithstanding the fact that she'd moved on and moved away and was now married to someone else.

But Serena had a habit of falling for men who were emotionally unavailable. Before Bobby Ray Ellis, she'd dated Howard Shelton, a widower with a gorgeous labradoodle. Before Howard, she'd gone out with Kevin Nolan, an attorney from Kalispell who'd been so focused on his billable hours he'd rarely had any time left for her.

And since she was thinking about time, she glanced at the clock and realized she didn't have much before Bailey was due to arrive.

"I've gotta go, Grams, but I'll call you next week," she promised.

As she hung up the phone, she couldn't help but wonder if she was making the same mistake with Bailey that she'd made so many times previously.

She knew that he had an ex-wife, but she didn't know any other details about his marriage or why it had ended. Was he still in love with the woman he'd married? Was her growing infatuation with the sexy cowboy going to end with more heartache?

Possibly…and yet, she couldn't stop her

heart from doing a happy little dance when she saw Bailey's truck pull up in front of her building now.

Chapter Eight

Bailey had called Serena on Friday night to confirm their plans for shopping the next day— and to offer to drive. She'd teasingly accused him of being worried that she might actually leave him at the mall, but she didn't oppose his plan. She did, however, request a slight detour when he picked her up Saturday morning.

"I have to stop at Crawford's before we head out," she told him, as she buckled her seat belt.

"You don't think that whatever you need

from the general store could be picked up in Kalispell?"

"No, because what I need is a tag from the Tree of Hope."

He looked at her blankly. "The what?"

"The Tree of Hope," she said again. "It was Nina's idea," she said, referring to the woman who'd been born a Crawford but was now married to Dallas Traub, with whom she was raising his three sons and her daughter. "It started about five years ago, when families were struggling to recover from the catastrophic flooding that summer, and so many people had nothing left to put presents under a Christmas tree—if they even had a Christmas tree."

She went on to explain that gift tags marked with the age and gender of the intended recipient were hung on the branches of a decorated tree inside Crawford's General Store. Customers would choose one or more of the tags, purchase appropriate gifts and return them to the store with the tags. Then Nina—and any other volunteers that she managed to recruit—would wrap and deliver the gifts.

"Rust Creek Falls really does take care of its own," Bailey noted, pulling into a parking spot near the General Store.

"Sometimes we need a little help from our neighbors," Serena acknowledged, unbuckling her belt. "After the flood, we were fortunate that a lot of folks from Thunder Canyon came to town to help with the cleanup and rebuild."

"That's the second time you've mentioned a flood," he observed as he opened her door for her.

"I guess the news didn't make its way down to New Mexico."

"I guess not," he confirmed.

"It was five years ago, around the Fourth of July. There were torrential rains in the area, and a lot of homes were ruined by the floods. Several public buildings were destroyed, the

Commercial Street Bridge was washed away, the Main Street Bridge was impassable, and Hunter McGee, the former mayor, died of a heart attack after a tree crushed the front of his car. That led to a battle between Collin Traub and Nate Crawford to fill the vacant office which, you could probably guess, Collin won, as he's still the mayor today."

"I had no idea about any of this," Bailey confessed.

"The devastation was unlike anything I've ever seen," she told him. "Afterward everyone pitched in to help with the cleanup and rebuild, but it still took months. And that," she said, passing through the door he held open for her and entering the store, "is the not-so-short story about the floods that led to the creation of the Tree of Hope."

Bailey followed Serena to the holiday display and the tree that appeared to be empty of tags.

On closer inspection, he found two. "There are only a couple of tags left."

"It is only a couple of weeks until Christmas," she pointed out.

He reached for the nearest tag and removed it from the branch to read the information on the back. "Male, seventy-two-years, diabetic, shoe size ten."

"There are some older residents in town who don't have any family around to celebrate with, so Nina added them to the Tree of Hope to ensure they aren't forgotten during the holidays."

"Do you think you can help me find a gift for a seventy-two-year-old diabetic man who wears a size ten?"

"Sugar-free candy and warm slippers," she immediately suggested.

He nodded and held on to the tag.

Serena took the last one from the tree.

"What did you get?" he asked.

"Seven-year-old boy." She approached Natalie Crawford, who was organizing a display of building block sets nearby. "Did Nina happen to put a tag from the Tree of Hope aside for me?"

"Oh, hi, Serena," Natalie said. "And yes, she did." She finished stacking the boxes in her hand, then moved toward the cash register. Opening a drawer beneath the counter, she retrieved a tag that had been stored there for safekeeping. "Here you go."

"Thanks." Serena slid both tags into the side pocket of her handbag, then turned back to Bailey. "Now we can go."

"Are you going to tell me what that was about?" Bailey asked, when they were back in his truck and en route to Kalispell.

"You mean the tag that Natalie gave me?" Serena guessed.

He nodded.

"If there's a three-year-old girl who needs a

gift, Nina will put that tag aside for me," she confided. "I know it's silly, but—"

"No," he interjected. "It's not silly at all. It's a good way to remember your sister at the holidays, at least until you find her again."

She was grateful for his understanding—and his confident assertion that she would one day be reunited with her sister. But she'd been hoping for exactly that for so long, she knew she had to accept the possibility that it might never happen. "*If* I ever do," she clarified.

"I didn't think I'd ever come back to Rust Creek Falls," he reminded her. "But here I am."

"And your family's thrilled to have you home," she said.

"I don't know about that, but it has been good to reconnect with most of my siblings. I haven't been able to spend much time with Dana, of course, because she's still living in Oregon with her adoptive family," he noted. "And we still don't know where Liza is, though Hudson's private investigator insists he's making progress."

"You don't believe him?"

He shrugged. "I think if I were a PI with a client whose pockets were as deep as Bella's husband's, I'd want to stay on his payroll, too."

"I don't think Hudson Jones is foolish enough to pay someone without results," she told him.

"You're probably right," he acknowledged. "But I know Bella would feel a lot better if she actually saw results, preferably in the form of our youngest sister."

"I'm sure you'll *all* feel better when you find Liza," she said, as he pulled into the parking lot of the shopping mall. "But right now, you need to focus on finding an empty parking spot."

"I hate Christmas shopping," Bailey announced several hours later as he followed Serena up to her apartment, his arms heavy with the weight of the bags he carried.

"What is it that you hate?" she asked, as she slid her key into the lock. "The festive decorations? The seasonal music? The shopkeepers wishing you happy holidays?"

"The crazy drivers racing for limited parking spots, the desperate shoppers pawing through boxes of toys and piles of clothes, then pressing toward the cash registers like teenage girls rushing the stage at a Justin Bieber concert."

She smiled at the image painted by his words as she carefully sidestepped an excited Marvin, who seemed determined to get tangled up in her feet.

"The key," she told him, "is not to let yourself get caught up in the chaos."

"Easy to say, not so easy to do when the chaos is all around."

"But you can't deny it was a successful day."

He unloaded his shopping bags on the floor, then dropped to his knees to give Marvin some of the attention he was begging for. "Except that apparently I now have to wrap all that stuff."

"Yes, you do," she confirmed. "But you'll see that I already have a wrapping station set up on the table, so you can get started while I heat up the sauce and put a pot of water on to boil for the pasta."

"Or I could make the spaghetti and you could do the wrapping?" he suggested as an alternative.

She shook her head. "I'll help you *after* dinner."

Marvin, even in a fog of canine euphoria induced by Bailey's belly rub, recognized that last word and immediately scrambled to his feet and raced over to his bowl.

Bailey chuckled.

"Yes, it's almost time for your dinner, too," she assured the eager bulldog. "Although I doubt you've worked up much of an appetite, hanging around inside the apartment all day."

"He could probably use some exercise," Bailey decided. "Do you want me to take him out for a walk before dinner?"

Poor Marvin didn't know whether to lie down and feign exhaustion—his usual response to hearing the word *walk*—or remain seated by his bowl in anticipation of his *dinner.*

Serena shook her head. "If you'd really rather *w-a-l-k* the dog than wrap presents, his leash and sweater are on the hook by the door."

"Sweater?" he echoed dubiously.

"It's December, and his short hair doesn't do much to keep him warm."

Of course, Marvin hated the idea of the sweater as much as Bailey did, but with Serena's help, they managed to get it over the dog's head and his front legs through the appropriate holes.

When Serena returned to the kitchen to stir the sauce, Bailey clipped the leash onto his collar and said, "Let's go."

But Marvin did not want to go. In fact, he sat stubbornly on his butt and refused to move, even with Bailey tugging on the leash.

"I think your dog's broken," he said to Serena.

"He's not broken, he just hates the snow."

"You could have told me that when I first offered to take him out," he noted.

"I could have," she agreed, making no effort to hide her amusement. "But he really does need the exercise."

"Did you hear that, Marvin? You need the exercise."

Marvin dropped his head, as if ashamed, but his butt remained firmly planted on the floor.

So Bailey bent down and picked him up.

"Jeez, he's gotta weigh at least fifty pounds."

"Fifty-five at his last checkup," Serena told him.

"Well, at least I'll get some exercise hauling him down the stairs." Then to Marvin, he said,

"But when we hit street level, your paws are on the ground."

Whether or not Marvin understood any of that, Bailey had no idea, but for now, the dog snuggled into the crook of his arm to enjoy the ride.

Serena held up her end of the bargain.

After Bailey and Marvin returned from their walk and the humans and animals had eaten, she helped him wrap the presents he'd bought.

Their efforts were occasionally impeded by her pets. Molly's curiosity about Bailey finally proved stronger than her wariness of strangers, and she ventured out from hiding to jump from chair to chair—and occasionally even onto the table—and knock various items onto the ground. Max somehow got tangled up in a length of curling ribbon, but after Serena untangled him, he mostly stayed out of the way, content to nibble on an empty wrapping paper tube. Marvin was the worst offender. Despite his pre-dinner walk with Bailey—who assured her that yes, he did make the dog walk—he remained full of energy and determined to cause mischief.

When Bailey folded the sweater he'd chosen for Bella and positioned it in the center of the paper he'd already cut, Serena shook her head.

"What?" he asked.

"You need a box."

"Why?"

"Because clothing should always go in a box—and because boxes are easier to wrap," she explained.

"You didn't make me put the pj's I bought for the triplets in boxes."

"Because you want kids' presents to be easy to open," she explained.

"There seem to be an awful lot of rules about gift-wrapping," he noted. "Maybe you should write them down for me."

She selected an appropriate-size box from her stock, lined it with tissue, refolded the sweater—after removing the price tag—laid it inside the box, closed the lid and handed it back to him.

He wrapped the paper around the box and fastened it with a piece of tape.

Serena picked up the gift she'd finished wrapping and looked beneath it, then under the table. "Did you take that bow?"

"What bow?"

"I had a green bow that I was going to put on this one."

"You have a whole box of bows," he pointed out.

"And I picked a green one out of the box and set it on the table right here," she said, indicating the spot. Then a movement caught her eye and she sighed. "Molly."

Bailey glanced over to see the cat in the middle of the living room, batting the missing bow around the floor.

Serena stepped away from the table just as Marvin decided to race ahead of her, knocking her off balance. Bailey instinctively reached for her—his arms wrapping around her and hauling her against him.

"Sorry." Her cheeks burned with embarrassment over her clumsiness, and her breasts—crushed against his chest now—tingled with awareness and arousal.

"I'm not," he said huskily, his arms still around her.

Then he lowered his head and touched his lips to hers.

Maybe she should have resisted the seductive pressure and the intoxicating flavor of his kiss. But the moment his mouth made contact with hers, her only thoughts were:

Yes.

This.

And, *More.*

He gave her more.

Parting her lips with his tongue, he deepened the kiss. He slid his hands down her back, then beneath the hem of her sweater. She shivered as his callused palms moved over her bare skin, an instinctive reaction that caused her breasts to rub against his hard chest, sending arrows of pleasure from her peaked nipples to her core.

He nibbled playfully on her lips, teased her with strokes of his tongue that made her tremble and ache with want. Her whole body felt hot, so hot she was sure her bones would melt.

And then he abruptly tore his mouth from hers. "What the—"

She drew in a slow deep breath and willed her head to stop spinning. "What?"

He looked down at his feet, where Molly was innocently licking her paw and rubbing it over her face.

But Serena knew better. "Molly," she said reprovingly.

"I think she left her claws in my skin," Bailey said.

"She's not overly fond of strangers," she admitted. "And she is somewhat protective of me."

He reached down to rub his shin. "Well, it's going to take a bigger cat than that to scare me away," he promised.

"Maybe she did us a favor," Serena suggested.

"I'm not feeling grateful."

"But we agreed we weren't going to do this," she reminded him.

"Why was that again?"

"Because neither one of us has had much success with relationships."

"That's true," he acknowledged. "And while I know I'm not so good with the opening up and sharing my emotions part, I promise you that I can muddle through the naked physical activity part."

"You sure do know how to tempt a girl, don't you?"

"Are you saying that you're *not* tempted?"

"I'm more tempted than I should be," she confessed.

"Obviously not tempted enough or we'd be doing it instead of talking about it," he told her.

"You've still got presents to wrap," she reminded him.

"I'd rather unwrap *you.*"

The words were accompanied by a heated look that made her knees weak—and her resolve even weaker. She consciously steeled both, picked up a roll of paper and pointed it at him. "Wrap."

Bailey took the paper—and the hint.

He was undeniably disappointed that she'd put on the brakes *again*, but he didn't really blame her. Although they'd spent a lot of time together over the past week, they'd really only known each other a week.

So while Serena went to retrieve the bow Molly had stolen, he tried to focus on measuring and cutting the paper—and not stare at the sexy curve of her butt.

"Tell me about your marriage," she suggested, as she affixed the bow to the wrapped gift.

"Well, that question effectively killed the mood," he noted.

"That wasn't my intention."

"Are you sure? Maybe you want to hear about all the reasons my marriage failed so that you can feel justified in pushing me away."

"I'm not pushing you away," she said. "But I'm also not in the habit of jumping into bed with a man I just met."

"I've told you more about me than a lot of other people know," he confided.

"So why won't you tell me about your marriage?"

He shrugged to indicate his surrender. "What do you want to know?"

"How long were you married?"

"Almost two years. And before you say, 'that's not very long,' believe me, it was long enough for both of us to know it wasn't working."

"I'm sorry. I didn't mean to pry. I didn't realize it was such a touchy subject."

He sighed. "It's not really. I just don't like admitting that I failed—and it was my failure. Because from the day we exchanged vows, I was waiting for everything to fall apart."

"Why were you so sure that it would?"

He shrugged. "Maybe because of what happened to my parents."

"They were killed by a drunk driver."

"Yeah," he acknowledged. "And before that, they were happy together, running the farm and raising a family. And then everything changed."

"Because of a tragic accident."

"Because of *me*," he said.

Serena frowned. "What are you talking about?"

"It was my fault they were on that particular road at that particular time on that particular night."

And he proceeded to tell her about the events of that fateful evening. How his older brother had invited him to go to an out-of-town bar. Although Bailey wasn't yet of legal drinking age, Luke assured him that he knew of a honky-tonk dive that didn't care if their customers had ID so long as they had cash to pay for their beer. Bailey was always happy to tag along with his brother, and when Danny heard they were going out, he refused to be left behind.

The bartender didn't blink when Luke ordered a pitcher of beer and three glasses, which he carried over to the table where his brothers waited. But Danny, always a rule follower, went back to the bar to get a soda.

When Bailey had emptied the pitcher into his glass, Danny suggested that they leave and asked for the keys. Bailey, who had driven, refused, unwilling to let his little brother call the shots. Besides, a trio of young women had just settled around the neighboring table and immediately began to chat up the three cowboys.

"But Danny—devoted to Annie—was even less interested in flirting than in drinking," Bailey continued his explanation. "And when me and Luke refused to heed his warnings and pleas, he went to the pay phone outside and called our parents."

Even after so many years, the memories were clear, the pain sharp. Everything had changed that night. Not just for Bailey, Luke and Danny, but their four younger siblings—and especially their parents.

"They were on their way to get you," Serena realized.

He nodded. "Because I was too stubborn, too arrogant, to let my little brother have the keys."

"And you've been carrying the guilt of that decision for more than a dozen years," she realized.

"Because it was *my* decision."

"It was your decision to hold on to the keys," she acknowledged. "And Danny's decision to call your parents. And their decision to come after you. But the only one responsible for their deaths is the drunk driver who hit them."

"So why can't I let go of the feeling that it's my fault?"

Chapter Nine

Serena understood guilt. She'd carried her fair share of it for a lot of years, and though she'd managed to let go of most of it, there were still moments that she wondered *what if,* still occasions when she felt sharp pangs of regret. So she wasn't going to tell Bailey to "let it go" and expect that he'd be able to do so. She knew it wasn't that easy, but she also knew that holding dark and negative feelings inside only strengthened their hold.

"I don't know," she said. "But I do know that talking about it can sometimes help."

"Like I said, I'm not good with the sharing feelings thing," he reminded her.

"Like anything else, it gets easier with practice," she promised.

"I don't know that that's true," he said. "But I do know that I find it easy to talk to you."

"I'm glad."

"In fact, all that stuff I just told you, about the night my parents were killed... I never told Emily," he confided.

"Why not?" she wondered aloud.

"When she asked about my family, I told her that my parents were dead and my siblings were scattered—though even I didn't know how scattered at that point. And she didn't seem interested in knowing anything more." He shrugged. "Probably because she was so close to her family, and me not having a family simplified our life. There was never any question about where we would spend the holidays—always with her family."

"How were those holidays?" Serena asked carefully.

"Fine," he said.

"Why is it, whenever someone gives that answer, it usually means not fine?"

"No, it was fine," he insisted. "I mean, I never got into the celebrations, but that was my fault. I had disconnected from my family and I didn't know how—or maybe I didn't want—to connect with hers."

"Did that become a source of friction between you?"

He shook his head. "There really wasn't friction between us. There really wasn't much of anything. In fact, I'm not even sure she noticed that I didn't connect with her family."

Now it was Serena's turn to frown. "What do you mean, she didn't notice?"

"She was the youngest of three kids and the

only girl, Daddy's little princess and her mother's best friend, doted on by her brothers, close with both of their wives and a favorite aunt to the kids. She was accustomed to being the center of attention and basked in that attention.

"It all came to a head when her youngest brother's wife had their first baby. We, of course, raced over to the hospital to celebrate the big event, and Emily immediately fell in love with her new niece. I braced myself for what I knew was coming next—or what I thought was coming next."

Serena nodded, undoubtedly anticipating the same response that he had.

"She looked at her brother and sister-in-law with their newborn and said, 'That's what I want.' A baby, I guessed, having resigned myself to that eventuality, because after marriage comes kids, right? Well, not always in that order," he acknowledged, responding to his own question. "But she surprised me by shaking her head. 'Yes, I want a baby,' she told me. 'But I want more than that.'

"Of course, I'm not very good at reading between the lines, so I said, 'You mean, two kids?' 'No, I mean the whole package,' she said. 'I want a husband who looks at me the way Matt looks at Tanya. A husband who wants to have a baby with me because he knows that child will be the best of both of us and a bond that ties us together forever.'

"Or words to that effect," Bailey said. "The point was, we both knew that husband wasn't ever going to be me. And that was the end."

"Are things better now?" Serena asked.

"If you consider being divorced better," he said dryly.

"I meant, are you both satisfied with the decision to end your marriage?" she clarified.

"I assume so," he said. "I haven't seen or spoken to her since I filed the divorce papers three years ago."

"You haven't had any contact with her in three *years*?"

"I thought a clean break would be best," he confided.

"I think you need to talk to her," Serena said. "And she probably needs to talk to you."

"Why?"

"For closure."

He scowled. "What does that even mean?"

"It means understanding how and why the relationship ended, so that you can accept that it has ended and move on," she explained patiently.

"We're divorced," Bailey reminded her. "I don't think either of us is under any illusions that the relationship isn't over."

"But have you moved on?" she prompted gently.

"I'd say the fourteen hundred miles I moved proves that I have."

"Have you dated much since the divorce?"

"Not really," he admitted.

"That's a rather vague response."

"Do you want to know the specific number of dates?"

"A range would suffice," she said.

"Then I guess it would be…more than zero and less than two," he confided.

"Only one?" she asked, surprised.

"And only if we're counting this as a date."

"This is a date?"

"Well, it was prearranged, I picked you up, we shared a meal—and a kiss. Doesn't that tick all the boxes?"

"I guess it does," she said, though she still sounded dubious.

"Or we could say it's not a date."

"I don't have a problem with the label," she said. "I'm just not sure how I feel about being your rebound girl."

"It's been three years," he reminded her. "I'm not on the rebound."

"Three years of not dating suggests you might have been more heartbroken over the failure of your marriage than you wanted to admit."

"Or maybe I'd finally accepted that I was so damaged by the mistakes of my past that I had nothing left to offer a woman."

"So what's changed to make you want to start dating again now?" she wondered aloud.

"I met you."

Those three simple words melted Serena's heart.

She was still thinking about them the next day as she slid the last tray of sugar cookies into the oven. Marvin, who'd been snoring in the corner, suddenly picked his head up, his ears twitching.

"Do you hear something?" she asked him.

He responded by leaping off his bed and racing toward the door. Serena wiped her hands on a towel and followed the dog, pulling open the door before she heard a knock.

"This is a surprise," she said, when she saw Bailey standing there.

"I left a message on your voice mail and sent a couple of texts, but you didn't respond, so I thought I'd take a chance and swing by after I ran some errands," he explained.

She stepped away from the door so that he could enter. "That's strange—I didn't hear my phone ring at all." And then a thought occurred to her. "Of course, I didn't plug it in last night, so chances are, the battery's dead."

"Is it okay that I stopped by?"

"Well, Marvin's certainly happy to see you," she said, with a pointed glance at the dog who had rolled over to display his belly.

Bailey chuckled as he bent down to give her pet a one-handed belly scratch. His other hand held up a padded envelope. "When I got home last night, this was on my doorstep."

"What is it?" she asked him.

"Another Christmas present that I need to wrap—and that I'm hoping you'll deliver for me."

She took the envelope and peeked inside. "You got a PKT-79?"

"Two of them," he told her. "For Owen and his friend Riley."

"I can't believe you managed to get your hands on not just one but two of the most popular toys of the season," she said.

"I took your advice," he admitted.

"eBay?"

He nodded.

"I'm not going to ask what these cost you."

"Good, because I'm not going to tell you," he said.

"You do know this wasn't necessary, right?"

"I know," he confirmed. "But it was something I wanted to do."

"It will definitely restore Owen's faith in Santa Claus," Serena murmured.

"I hope so," Bailey said. "Because spending time with you seems to be restoring my faith in the spirit of the season."

She smiled at that. "All the wrapping stuff is still on the table—I haven't got around to putting it away yet."

"It looks like you've been busy with other things," he said, glancing around the kitchen. Then he lifted his head and sniffed the air. "Cookies?" he asked hopefully.

She nodded. "But nothing as fancy as your sister-in-law makes."

"Cookies don't need to be fancy to taste good," he noted, as he washed his hands at the sink.

She lifted one off the cooling rack and offered it to him.

He picked up a towel to dry his hands, but

instead of taking the cookie from her, he lowered his head and bit a piece off.

"Mmm," he said around a mouthful of cookie. "That is good." Then he took another bite, and another, until he was nipping at her fingers, the teasing nibbles making her blood pulse and her knees weak.

She took a step back and wiped her hands down the front of her apron, brushing the crumbs away.

He grinned, no doubt aware of the effect he had on her.

"So," he said, moving over to the table and selecting a roll of wrapping paper, "what are your plans for the rest of the afternoon?"

"The afternoon's almost over," she pointed out to him.

"Okay, what are your plans for tonight?"

The oven timer buzzed and she slid her hands into the padded mitts and retrieved the hot tray of cookies.

"After I get the kitchen cleaned up, I'm going to pop a big bowl of popcorn and snuggle up on the sofa with Marvin, Molly and Max to watch one of my favorite holiday movies."

"I don't see Molly as a snuggler," he said. "Of course, that might be because I can still feel her claws digging into my leg."

"She really is a sweetheart, once you get to know her."

He snorted, a clear expression of disbelief.

Serena filled the sink with hot soapy water and began washing her dishes.

"You didn't mention any plans for dinner," Bailey commented as he finished taping his present.

"I figured I'd skip dinner, because I've been sampling cookies all day," she confided.

"Or I could go over to the Ace and pick up burgers."

"I really don't need a burger." But now that

he'd put the idea in her head, her mouth was watering.

"But do you want one?" Bailey asked, his tone suggesting that he already knew the answer.

"Now I do," she admitted.

"Fries?"

"No," she said firmly.

He chuckled. "Okay, just a burger."

"Cheeseburger," she clarified.

"Anything else?"

She started to shake her head, then paused. "Yeah—why are you doing this?"

"Because I'm hungry?" he suggested.

"I don't just mean the food. I mean why are you here?"

He held up the package he'd finished wrapping.

"You expect me to believe that Eva didn't have wrapping paper?" she asked.

"Okay, so maybe that was just an excuse to see you."

"You shouldn't need an excuse to visit a friend," she told him.

He sighed. "You're still determined to stick me in that friend zone, aren't you?"

"I think friendship is always a good place to start."

To start what? Bailey wanted to know.

But he didn't ask the question. He had no right to demand answers from Serena about the status or direction of their relationship when he hadn't yet figured out what he wanted.

But he knew that he wanted *her*. And the more time he spent with her, the stronger the wanting grew.

A smart man would realize that the key to getting a woman out of his head—and his hormones back in check—would be to put some distance between them. A smart man would have ignored the impulse that drove him into town and then steered him toward her apartment.

Apparently he was not a smart man.

Instead, he picked up burgers—and fries for himself—from the Ace in the Hole. When he got back to Serena's apartment, Marvin went nuts all over again, as if Bailey had been gone for days rather than forty minutes.

Growing up, there had always been a dog or two at Sunshine Farm and several cats hanging around the barn, but Bailey hadn't had a pet since he'd left Rust Creek Falls thirteen years earlier. He hadn't wanted the responsibility. But he was beginning to see how much joy an animal companion could add to life—at least an animal like Marvin. He was still skeptical about Molly and undecided on Max, who mostly kept to himself.

While he was gone, Serena had cleared off the dining room table so they had somewhere to sit and eat. Then Bailey took Marvin outside while she made popcorn and set up the movie.

He hadn't asked what they would be watching—because it really didn't matter. He just wanted to hang out with her, and if that meant watching Bing Crosby and Danny Kaye sing and dance with Rosemary Clooney and Vera-Ellen, so be it.

He was admittedly surprised when, instead of the instrumental notes of a classic Irving Berlin song, the screen filled with an image of an airplane coming in for a landing against the backdrop of an orange sky.

"*Die Hard* is your favorite Christmas movie?" he asked. *"Really?"*

"It's a Christmas classic."

"I don't disagree."

"But you thought I'd want to watch *White Christmas*," she guessed.

"Maybe," he acknowledged, happy to be proven wrong.

He settled on the sofa, the bowl of popcorn in his lap. Marvin scrambled up onto the sofa beside Serena and promptly fell asleep. Max positioned himself by her feet, where he nibbled on a carrot-shaped pet chew. Molly was apparently in hiding, which didn't hurt Bailey's feelings at all and allowed him to focus on the woman seated beside him.

Because he sure as heck couldn't focus on the movie—not with Serena so close. Not when his fingers brushed against hers every time he reached into the bowl. Not when her hair tickled his chin when she tipped her head back. And definitely not when he inhaled her tantalizing scent with every breath he took.

But the woman who was the center of his attention seemed oblivious, her gaze fixed on the movie. When only a few unpopped kernels remained in the bottom of the bowl and the first staccato bursts of gunfire erupted on the screen, Molly sauntered into the living room, the tip of her tail high in the air, flicking side to side.

The cat made her way toward the sofa, then froze, her pale green eyes narrowing to slits. Apparently Bailey was in her spot, and she wasn't happy about it, as evidenced by the way she hissed at him.

"Molly!" Serena scolded.

The cat continued to stare at him, unaffected by the reprimand.

"I'm sorry," Serena apologized. "She's never…okay, not never…but she rarely does that." Her brow furrowed as she considered. "And it's only ever been when I have male company—which isn't very often," she hastened to add.

"She's protective of you," he said, echoing her earlier remark.

She glanced at the snoring lump pressed against her thigh. "Unlike Marvin, who would sell me out for a belly rub."

Bailey chuckled at that.

Serena leaned over to scoop up the cat, holding her so that she was nose to nose with the feline.

"Bailey is our friend," she said, her tone firm but gentle. "And you need to be nice to our friends. No biting, no scratching, no growling, no hissing."

The demon cat gently bumped her nose against Serena's, then rubbed her face against her cheek—and actually purred.

"I told you she can be affectionate," she said.

"Is she really being affectionate?" he wondered aloud. "Or is she just gloating?"

"What?"

"She's cuddling up to you but looking at me, as if to rub it in that she's your favorite."

Serena laughed at that. "Do you feel as if you're in competition with my cat?"

"Well, I can't help but notice that she's a lot closer to you than you've let me get."

"Molly's been with me eleven years," she reminded him. "I've known you just over a week."

"I hope you're not suggesting that it's going to take me another ten years and fifty-one weeks to get to second base."

She shook her head, but a smile tugged at her lips. "I'm suggesting that we should watch the rest of the movie."

So they did. But it seemed all too soon that the credits were rolling on the screen, and Bailey knew it was time to say good-night and head back to his cold empty cabin at Sunshine Farm. His reluctance was a little unnerving. He was accustomed to being on his own and had always been content that way. Now it seemed that he might prefer Serena's company—and possibly even that of her furry menagerie.

"Thanks for letting me hang out with you tonight," he said when she walked him to the door.

"It was fun," she agreed.

"Maybe we could do it again next weekend,"

he suggested. "But instead of staying in, we could go out for dinner and a movie."

"I'd like that," she said. "Although this time of year, movie nights at the high school generally feature holiday films."

"Or we could drive into Kalispell and see a new release in a real theater."

"That sounds a lot like a date," she mused.

"It does tick all the boxes," he confirmed. "What time do you finish work on Friday?"

"Four o'clock."

"I'll pick you up at six," he said, already counting the hours.

Amanda Langley was seated inside Daisy's Donut Shop when Serena arrived to meet her at noon on Friday. They'd chosen the restaurant because of its proximity to the veterinarian clinic as Serena only had an hour for lunch—and because the food was as good as the service was prompt.

"I'm glad you were available to meet me

today," she said to her mom, as she slid into the seat across from her.

"I was grateful for the invitation," Amanda replied.

Serena set aside her menu. She ate at Daisy's often enough that she already knew what she wanted, and the waitress immediately appeared to take their orders.

"I wanted to apologize to you," Serena said when the server had gone.

"Apologize?" Amanda echoed, sounding surprised. "For what?"

"Interrupting your date last Saturday night."

Her mother waved a hand dismissively. "It was fine. And Mark was glad that he finally got to meet you."

"So you did tell him about me?"

"I've told him everything," Amanda assured her.

"You have?"

Her mother nodded. "I've learned that keeping things inside isn't good for me—and that I need to stop doing things that aren't good for me." Then she smiled. "Mark is very good for me."

Serena chose to ignore the obvious implication, saying only, "Well… I'm glad you have someone you can talk to."

"Do you? Have someone that you can talk to, I mean?"

"Sure," she said, because she knew it was true. It was also true that she didn't usually like to talk about the past.

And yet, for some reason, she'd had no trouble opening up to Bailey. In fact, she'd *wanted* to tell him about Mimi. But even more surprising was the realization that he was a good listener. Understanding and empathetic.

And a really great kisser.

Of course, that probably wasn't something she should be thinking about right now. Not just because she was having lunch with her mother, but because she was the one who had told him that they should slow things down. Although she was admittedly a little disappointed that he hadn't tried to kiss her goodbye when he'd left her apartment the other night.

"It's still so hard, not knowing," Amanda said.

The softly spoken remark drew Serena back to the present. She nodded, understanding that her mother was thinking about Mimi and that tragic day when she'd gone missing.

"There are so many possibilities…most of them too horrible to think about," her mother noted.

"So don't think about them," she urged.

"I try not to," Amanda admitted. "I want to believe that she was taken by somebody—a woman or even a couple—who desperately wanted a child but couldn't have one of their own. And maybe it seemed unfair, that I had two beautiful little girls—" she lifted her napkin to dab at the tears that trembled on her lashes "—so they took one home."

It was the same scenario that Serena clung to—the one that allowed her to sleep at night. It couldn't change the fact that her sister had been cruelly ripped from the arms of her loving family, but she desperately needed to believe that, wherever she was now, Mimi was loved and cared for and didn't miss her real family at all.

She reached across the table and touched her mother's hand.

"She was such a sweet child," Amanda said, turning her palm over to clasp her daughter's hand.

Serena nodded, feeling as if their joined hands were squeezing her heart.

"I should have held on to her tighter," her mother said.

"I was—" Serena swallowed. "I was holding Mimi's hand," she reminded Amanda.

Her mother's brow furrowed, as if she was struggling to remember, then she shook her head. "You were a child yourself. I never should have made you responsible for your sister."

"I thought you blamed me," she said. "I thought that's why…"

"Why I turned into an alcoholic?" Amanda guessed.

She nodded again.

"I hate knowing that you could ever believe such a thing," her mother said, her eyes bright with unshed tears. "That I ever let you believe such a thing."

"I blamed myself," Serena confided.

"It wasn't your fault. Please tell me you know that none of what happened was your fault," Amanda implored.

"I do know. Now," she said. "Most of the time, anyway."

Her mother gave Serena's hand a gentle

squeeze before releasing it as the waitress approached with their plates.

"You were the only light in my darkest days," Amanda said when the server had gone. "You were never responsible for any of the wrong choices I made, but you were the biggest part of the reason why I was finally able to get sober."

"I didn't do anything," she said, and she'd always felt a little bit guilty about that.

"You always were, and still are, my sweet, beautiful daughter. And I want to earn the right to be your mother again, to be worthy of your love again."

"You always were, and still are, my mother. And I have always, and still do, love you," Serena told her.

Amanda's lips started to curve, then her smile wobbled. "Dammit," she said, and lifted her napkin to dab at the tears that trembled on her lashes. "I promised myself that I wasn't going to get weepy today."

Serena's own eyes were watery as she picked up her fork. "So tell me more about Mark," she said, suspecting they'd both appreciate a change in the topic of conversation.

"He's asked me to go with him tomorrow to cut down a Christmas tree," her mother said.

Serena sipped from her glass of water while she considered this information. For most people, it would be a traditional holiday event, but she knew that holiday events were often triggers for her mom.

"How do you feel about that?" she asked cautiously.

"Scared," Amanda admitted. "I find it's easier to get through the holidays if I pretend they don't exist."

"Not easy to do when the whole town is decked out in red and green," Serena noted.

"Well, apparently, the world does continue to turn through the whole month of December—at least for everyone else."

"You know, you can tell him no," she said. "If you're not ready."

"I've been saying no for the past three years," her mother confided. "I think it's time to say yes. I want you to know that I'm strong enough to say yes."

"Don't do this for me," Serena said. "Please."

"I'm not. I'm doing it for Mark, and for me. Okay, and maybe a little bit for you…and for Mimi."

Serena swallowed another sip of water—along with the lump in her throat. "Then you better get a huge tree and decorate it with hundreds of twinkling lights and tons of sparkly ornaments."

"We will," her mother promised.

And Serena trusted that they would.

Chapter Ten

There'd been plenty of chores around Sunshine Farm to keep Bailey's hands busy throughout the week, but the physical labor hadn't stopped him from thinking about Serena, wondering what she was doing and wishing he was with her instead of fixing fence, moving hay or cleaning tack. But he knew that she was busy, too, with her responsibilities at the vet clinic, preparations for the holidays and, of course, her animals.

By Friday, he could hardly wait for their date

that night. In the afternoon, he slipped away from the ranch for a few hours to meet Brendan Tanner at the community center.

"This town is truly amazing," Brendan remarked, after they'd sorted through the gifts that had been donated for Presents for Patriots.

"You must not get out much," Bailey said dryly.

The other man chuckled. "I've been to a lot of places—bigger cities, prettier towns." He sighed wistfully. "Places with pizza delivery."

"There is something to be said for the luxury of food brought to your door," Bailey agreed.

"On the other hand, people who don't have that option are forced to go out and interact with other people," Brendan noted. "Maybe that's why there's such a strong sense of community in Rust Creek Falls."

"I don't think pizza delivery would jeopardize the town's identity."

"It's something to think about, anyway," the retired marine said.

Bailey stood back and looked at the pile of gifts. "Where did all this stuff come from?"

"Rumor has it that Arthur Swinton donates the majority of these gifts every year," Brendan remarked.

"Since when do you put any stock in gossip?" Bailey asked.

His friend shrugged. "It seems to be a favorite pastime in this town."

"Because there's not much else to do."

"Well, it's a fact that Swinton bankrolled this whole place," Brendan told him, gesturing to their surroundings. "The Grace Traub Community Center was made possible by his generous support."

"Who is this Swinton guy?"

"The former mayor of Thunder Canyon who went to prison for embezzlement several years back."

"He built this place with stolen money?"

Brendan chuckled. "No, I'm pretty sure he paid that back."

Bailey was captivated by this tidbit, but he wasn't nearly as interested in history as he was the future. More specifically, his future plans with Serena. He surveyed all they'd accomplished. "Looks like we're done here. Is it okay if I take off?"

"Hot date tonight?" his friend teased.

"Just heading into Kalispell to grab a bite and catch a movie," he said, deliberately not answering the question.

"By yourself?"

"No," he admitted. "With…a friend."

"Serena Langley?" Brendan guessed.

"Yeah."

"I guess the rumor mill got that one right, too."

"I don't want to know," Bailey told him.

His friend chuckled again. "Well, have a good time tonight."

Bailey planned on it.

He'd made reservations at a popular steak and seafood restaurant in Kalispell and previewed the movie listings so they could discuss their options over dinner. He'd been looking forward to this date with Serena all week, and he hoped that she had been, too.

So he was understandably surprised when she opened the door in response to his knock and he saw that she was dressed in flannel pajamas with fuzzy slippers on her feet.

"I don't think the restaurant has a dress code, but considering that it's only twenty degrees outside, you might want to put on a pair of boots."

"Restaurant?" she echoed, then winced. "Oh, right. Dinner and a movie."

"You forgot our date," he realized, surprised and more than a little disappointed.

"I did. I'm sorry. It was just a really lousy day, and when I got home, all I wanted were my pj's. And ice cream," she admitted.

He looked closer, saw the puffiness lingering around her eyes. "You've been crying."

"I'm out of ice cream," she said, her eyes filling with fresh tears.

"You had lunch with your mom today," he suddenly remembered.

She nodded. "But that was fine. My mother's really doing well."

"So what happened after lunch?" he asked.

"Thelma McGee came in with Oreo," she said.

"I'm not yet seeing the connection between your tears and cookies," he confided.

She managed a smile as she shook her head. "Oreo is—*was*—Thelma's black-and-white cat."

The *was* finally clued him in to the cause of

her distress. He drew her into his arms, a silent offer of comfort.

She choked on a sob. "I'm sorry."

"There's no need to apologize," he assured her.

"Believe it or not, I'm getting better at dealing with the loss of an animal," she told him. "But it's never easy. And Thelma had Oreo for seventeen years."

"That's a pretty good life span for a cat, isn't it?"

"It is," she confirmed.

But he understood that when you loved something—or someone—and your time together came to an end, it was never long enough.

"She was sitting with him in the exam room, waiting for the doctor to come in, holding Oreo close to her chest, silent tears falling. And Oreo lifted a paw to her cheek, as if to comfort her."

Listening to Serena recount the story now, even he felt as if his chest was being squeezed.

He could only imagine how much more heart-wrenching it had been for her in the moment.

"I love my job," she told him.

Bailey continued to rub her back. "I know you do."

She sighed. "But sometimes... I really hate my job."

"That's understandable," he assured her.

She sniffled again. "I need a tissue."

He pulled one from the box on the sideboard, offered it to her.

"Thanks." She wiped her nose. "I can't believe I completely forgot about our plans for tonight."

"It's not too late, if you want to go put some clothes on."

"I'm sorry," she said again. "But I really don't feel up to going anywhere tonight."

"Do you feel up to company?" he asked.

"You want to stay?"

"Well, I know for a fact that you've got a decent movie collection. And popcorn."

"But no ice cream."

"Do you want me to go get you some ice cream?"

She nodded her head against his chest.

"What kind?"

"It doesn't matter, as long as it's real ice cream."

"I didn't know there was such a thing as fake ice cream," he told her.

"Low-fat ice cream, frozen yogurt, sorbet—they're all fake ice cream."

"I'll get the real stuff," he promised.

He wasn't gone long, and when he came back, he offered her a ribbon-tied paper bundle.

"I meant to pick up flowers for you earlier, but I forgot."

"At least you didn't forget our date," she said, as she unwrapped the bouquet of red carnations and white chrysanthemums with accents of red berries and seasonal greens. "And these are beautiful, thank you."

"My pleasure," he said.

"What else have you got there?" she asked, noting the two grocery bags he set on the counter.

"Ice cream."

"That's a lot of ice cream," she remarked.

"I picked up a couple frozen pizzas, too, in case you get hungry for food. That way, we won't have to go out." He opened the freezer and stowed the pizzas away, then unpacked the ice cream.

Four different flavors of ice cream: chocolate chip cookie dough, mint chocolate chip, black cherry and butterscotch ripple.

She took a couple bowls out of the cupboard, then retrieved spoons and a scoop from the utensil drawer.

"Why don't you scoop up the ice cream while

I put these flowers in some water?" she suggested.

He took the scoop she handed to him. "What kind do you want?"

"How am I supposed to decide when there are so many options?"

"A scoop of each?" he suggested.

"That would probably be a little overindulgent." She found a vase under the sink, filled it with water. "Maybe a little bit of mint chocolate chip and a little chocolate chip cookie dough."

While he dished up the ice cream, she snipped the stems off the flowers, arranged them in the vase, then set the bouquet in the center of the dining room table.

He handed her a bowl of ice cream. She noted that he'd gone for the butterscotch.

"Die Hard 2?" she suggested.

"Sounds good to me."

So they sat down with their ice cream and

prepared to watch Bruce Willis fight bad guys at Washington Dulles International Airport.

When the British jet crashed on the runway, Bailey caught a flickering motion in the corner of his eye and realized it was Molly's tail twitching from side to side. Apparently the cat had overcome her distrust of him, at least enough to climb up onto the table beside the sofa and lap the remnants of ice cream from his bowl.

"Is she allowed to have that?" he asked Serena.

"Do you want to take it away from her?" she countered.

"No," he admitted.

She smiled. "A little bit of ice cream isn't going to hurt her."

"But will it make her like me?"

"That remains to be seen."

"How about you?" he asked, sliding his arm

across her shoulders. "Did I earn points for feeding you ice cream?"

"You did." Then she dropped her head back against his chest and turned her attention back to the movie.

Though he'd wanted to take her out on a "real date" tonight, he realized that he was more than content to be here with her now. He couldn't remember ever feeling so comfortable and relaxed with his ex-wife. Emily was a social creature who'd always wanted to be going somewhere and doing something, and Bailey had almost forgotten that it could be fun just to relax.

"I'm going to preheat the oven for pizza," he said, after the hero had ejected himself from the cockpit of a plane.

"Why does it seem like you're always feeding me?" Serena asked when Bailey had completed his task and returned to his seat beside her.

"It's just frozen pizza."

She shifted slightly to face him. "Which doesn't answer my question," she pointed out.

He shrugged. "We seem to hang out together around meal times. And you made dinner for me after our shopping trip last week," he pointed out.

"That was once."

"Are we keeping score?" he asked, sounding amused.

"No." Then she revised her response, "Maybe."

He chuckled. "If you're really concerned about balancing the scales, you could offer to cook for me again sometime."

Serena considered this idea in conjunction with other thoughts nudging at her mind—and desires humming in her veins. "How about breakfast?" she suggested impulsively.

"Breakfast?" Bailey echoed.

"You know—the meal generally served in the morning," she clarified, her deliberately casual tone a marked contrast to the frantic beating of her heart. "Maybe after you've spent the night."

Heat supplanted the humor in his gaze. "When were you thinking you might make me this breakfast?"

The kisses they'd already shared assured her that the attraction she felt was reciprocated and gave her the courage to boldly respond, "Tomorrow."

Then, because she wanted him more than she wanted to watch a movie she'd seen a dozen times before, she breached the scant distance between them and touched her mouth to his.

That first contact was all it took to have desire pour through her system like molten lava, heating every part of her. What she'd intended to be a quick and easy kiss quickly changed, their mutual desire growing stronger and more intense. When he eased her back onto the sofa, she lifted her arms to link them behind his head, drawing him down with her, welcoming the weight of his body pressing her into the cushions. Her lips parted willingly when he deepened the kiss; her tongue dipped and dallied with his.

His hands skimmed down her sides, scorching her skin even through the fabric of her pajama top. She wanted to strip away her clothes and feel his hands on her bare skin; she wanted to strip away his clothes and use her hands on his bare skin. She wanted—

Beep-beep-beep.

Bailey drew in a ragged breath and eased away from her. "I better get that pizza in the oven."

After taking a moment to catch her own breath, Serena opened her eyes and found all three animals sitting in a row, staring at her.

"You have no right to judge me," she told them, reaching for the remote to pause the movie.

"Especially you," she said, pointing the control at Marvin. "Because you'd show your private parts to anyone for a belly rub." He pressed his wet nose to her leg, an acknowledgment more than an apology.

"And you act like you don't like him," she said to Molly. "But that didn't stop you from licking his ice cream bowl." The calico lifted her butt in the air and extended her front paws out in front of her, stretching lazily.

Max looked at her, his nose twitching. She gently scratched behind his ears. "And you'll cuddle with anyone, in your own time and on your own terms."

"Were you talking to me?" Bailey asked, returning to the living room.

"No," she said.

Thankfully he didn't require more of an explanation as he settled beside her on the sofa again. And though the press of his thigh against hers was enough to jolt her pulse again, she hit the play button to resume the movie.

Twenty minutes later, they were eating pizza and the animals were cowering from the noise of the firefight playing out on the TV screen.

And then they were kissing again.

She wasn't sure how it happened, or even who made the first move this time, she only knew that she didn't want him to ever stop kissing her. Or touching her.

She drew her knees up so they bracketed his hips, then lifted her pelvis to rub it against his. She could feel his erection straining against his jeans and gloried in the friction of the denim against her flannel pajama bottoms. He groaned softly as he ground into her, giving her a preview of what she wanted, what they both wanted.

She gasped with pleasure—then shock, as a wet doggy tongue swept across her cheek.

"Maybe we should move to the bedroom—and close the door," she suggested.

He stood up, as if eager to accept her invitation, and offered his hand to help her to her feet. But when she started to lead him down the hall, he paused.

"What's the matter?" she asked.

"You said you wanted to slow things down," he reminded her.

"That was last week. Ten days ago, in fact." She didn't want to slow down anymore. She wanted to move full speed ahead—with Bailey. She wanted his hands on her body. All over her body. And she wanted to explore every inch of his in return.

"I can't believe I'm saying this, but ten days isn't so long," he pointed out. "And if this happens tonight, I might worry afterward that it only happened because you were trying to balance the scales."

"If this happens tonight, it's because I want it to happen—not because you brought ice cream or pizza or even flowers," she assured him.

"You had a lousy day," he reminded her.

"I'm pretty sure getting naked with you would make me forget about the lousy day."

"I'm pretty sure getting naked with you would make me forget my name," he told her. "But it's not the answer."

But before he left, he kissed her goodbye.

It was a long, lingering kiss that assured her that he desired her as much as she desired him, despite his insistence on giving her time she no longer wanted or needed.

And when he finally drew away, she watched him go when she really wished she'd been able to convince him to stay.

Ten days before Christmas, volunteers gathered at the community center to wrap Presents for Patriots. The event was the culmination of many hours of work by many hands, and by seven o'clock, the room was bustling with activity and practically overflowing with volunteers.

For the residents of Rust Creek Falls, the annual gift-wrapping was very much a social occasion—a welcome opportunity to get together with their neighbors and catch up on what was going on. As Bailey looked around, he had to agree with Brendan's assessment: this was an amazing community.

More surprising to him was the number of people that he recognized from years ago and others whose acquaintance he'd made more recently. Mallory and Caleb Dalton were in attendance, as was Caleb's sister Paige with her husband, Sutter Traub. Will and Jordyn Clifton were working at a table alongside Will's brother Craig and his fiancée, Caroline Ruth. Claire and Levi Wyatt were at an adjacent table, Lani and Russ Campbell at another. Even the mayor and his wife had helped with the wrapping for a short while before they had to slip away to another holiday party.

At one point, Winona Cobbs popped in, and

while the eccentric psychic was sipping some of the complimentary hot apple cider, she told Bailey that his life was going to change before the night was over—but only if he was willing to let it. Everyone in town knew the old woman was more than a little odd, so Bailey tried not to let her words unnerve him.

Throughout the evening, he overheard some snippets of conversation and learned that Thelma McGee had already offered to foster cats for the animal shelter. She wasn't ready to replace her beloved Oreo, but she was eager to help out.

There were also murmurs, but no confirmation, that Paige and Sutter were expecting their second child, and that Paige's sister Lani was expecting her first.

There were sighs of relief, and some chuckles, when it was revealed that the heart attack that caused Melba Strickland to rush her husband, Gene, to the hospital in Kalispell turned out to be indigestion.

Christmas music played softly in the background throughout, and there was a refreshment table that offered not only hot apple cider but coffee, tea and hot cocoa, plus an assortment of seasonal cookies and treats—all donated by the generous folks of Rust Creek Falls. There was certainly plenty going on to keep the volunteers busy, and Bailey mostly hovered in the background.

Although he'd been involved in the planning and organization of the event almost from the beginning, he still felt like an outsider in the community. Of course, that was his own fault. He'd mostly resisted getting involved because, as he'd been reminding his family for almost twelve months, he didn't intend to stay.

And yet, he'd still made no plans to go.

He restocked the tables as wrapping supplies dwindled, collected finished packages and cleared away debris, and regularly found his attention shifting to the door. He told himself that he wasn't looking for anyone in particular, but when his gaze zeroed in on Serena and his heart bumped against his ribs, he was forced to acknowledge the truth.

He'd been watching for her.

And he'd been thinking about her almost non-stop since he'd declined the invitation to her bed. All the way home, after he'd kissed her goodbye at her door last night, he'd cursed himself for being a fool. It was little consolation to his aching body to know that he'd done the right thing. And he couldn't help but wonder if she'd ever give him another chance to make a different choice.

"I didn't see your name on the volunteer list," he said, after he'd crossed the room to meet her.

"Did you look for it?" she asked, a teasing glint in her eye.

He had, because he'd wanted to see her. And

now she was here, but he wasn't quite ready to put all his cards on the table. "I looked at all the names," he said.

"Then you know there were more than enough people signed up for the wrapping," she explained. "So I thought I'd come late to help with the cleaning."

"We had more than enough people sign up for that, too."

"I can see that," she acknowledged. "Are you going to send me away?"

"Of course not." Instead, he dipped his head and touched his mouth to hers. "I'm glad you're here."

The unexpected—and unexpectedly public—gesture surprised Serena. She'd wondered, after he'd left her apartment the night before, if she'd misinterpreted the situation. His kiss, in addition to making her lips tingle and spreading warmth through her veins, reassured her that she had not.

She smiled at him. "*That* made the walk over here totally worthwhile."

He drew back to look at her. "Why on earth would you walk over here in twenty-degree weather?"

"So that I could ask you for a ride home."

"I'd be happy to take you home," he assured her. "But I'm not sure how much longer I'm going to be stuck—"

"As of right now, you're unstuck," Brendan interjected, obviously having overheard at least part of their conversation. "Fiona already agreed to stick around and, no offense, but she's much prettier than you."

Bailey chuckled. "No offense taken, and Serena's much prettier than you, too, so I guess we both win."

Brendan held out his hand. "Thanks for all your help."

"It was my pleasure," Bailey said, clasping his hand and grasping his other shoulder.

Not quite a man-hug, but a gesture that spoke of the friendship and camaraderie that Serena guessed had developed between them over the past few months.

"Have you been here all day?" she asked, as she and Bailey exited the community center together.

"No, just since two," he said.

"Still, that's a lot of hours."

"Yeah, but it was a good day," he told her. "Being away from Rust Creek Falls for so long, I almost forgot what it was like to be part of such a tight-knit community."

"Did you miss it?"

"I didn't let myself," he admitted, opening the passenger door of his truck for her. "Not the town. And definitely not my family."

"Why did you finally come back?" she asked, when he was settled behind the steering wheel.

He turned the key in the ignition, then cranked the defroster to clear the windshield and warm up the truck's cab. "After my marriage fell apart, I was kind of at loose ends. I could have stayed in New Mexico, but I didn't want to, so I decided to make my way back to Wyoming, to see if I could track down Luke and Danny again.

"Of course, they were both gone by then, but the foreman at the ranch where Luke had last been working told me that he'd gone to Rusty River."

"Rusty River?" she echoed, amused by the bastardization of the town's name.

He shrugged. "Not a lot of people outside of Montana have heard of Rust Creek Falls, and the Rusty part was at least close enough that I was able to figure out where he'd gone—although I couldn't imagine why he'd want to come back to the town we'd said goodbye to forever."

"Well, whatever his reasons, I'm glad he came home," she said, as Bailey pulled into a vacant parking spot behind her building. "Because then you came home, too."

She unbuckled her belt, and he did the same, then came around to help her out of the truck.

"I didn't plan on staying—in Rust Creek Falls," he clarified, as they started up the steps to her apartment. "Even as the days turned into weeks and then months, I was sure I'd pack up and head out again."

"But you're still here," she noted.

"And right now, I don't want to be anywhere else."

She unlocked her door, then turned to face him. "Did you want to come in for hot cocoa and cookies?"

"I don't know," he said. "I seem to recall you once telling me that I needed to cut back on the Christmas cookies."

"I seem to recall that was an attempt to cover for your ill-tempered comment to a little boy."

"You don't think I need to worry about staying in shape?"

She splayed her palms on his chest. Even through his sheepskin-lined leather jacket, she could feel the hard strength of his muscles. "I don't think a couple of cookies are any cause for concern."

"What about the cocoa?"

She slid her hands over his shoulders to link them behind his head. "Maybe we should skip the cocoa," she said, and drew his mouth down to hers.

Chapter Eleven

They bypassed the kitchen and headed straight to her bedroom. On the way, Serena almost tripped over Marvin, who had eagerly raced ahead and jumped on the bed.

She sighed. "He thinks it's playtime."

"I was hoping the same thing," Bailey said. "But just between me and you."

She smiled at that, then turned to Marvin and in a firm tone said, "Off."

His excitement leaked out of him like air escaping from a punctured balloon, and he dropped his head and crawled to the edge of the mattress. He paused then, as if giving her an opportunity to rescind her banishment. Serena pointed to the door. Marvin reluctantly jumped down off the bed and retreated from the room.

"This is a new feeling for me," Bailey said.

"What's a new feeling?"

"I'm torn between the anticipation of finally getting you naked and guilt that you sent the dog away."

"If it makes you feel any better, I promise that Marvin doesn't hold a grudge. In fact, he's probably curled up on Molly's pillow already."

"So you're telling me it's okay to focus on the getting you naked part?"

"I'm suggesting we focus on getting one another naked," she said.

He smiled and pulled her into his arms. "That works for me."

Then he kissed her again. His tongue slid between her lips, to tease and tangle with hers.

His hands slid under her sweater, searching for skin, and found a soft cotton T-shirt instead.

"Damn Montana winters," he grumbled, as he yanked the shirt out of her jeans and finally put his hands on *her*. His callused palms moved over her skin, stroking her body, stoking her desire.

She fumbled with the buttons of his shirt, desperate to touch him as he was touching her, and discovered that he was wearing a thermal tee beneath. "Damn Montana winters," she echoed his complaint.

He chuckled as he yanked the shirt over his head and tossed it aside. The rest of their clothes quickly followed. Then he eased her down onto the mattress, covering her naked body with his own.

Her hands slid up his arms, tracing the muscular contours. Her palms stroked the shape of his bare shoulders, so broad, so strong. Then trailed over the hard planes of his chest and his stomach. He had the body of a rancher, lean and tough, and she wanted to lick every bit of it. But for now, she reached down and wrapped her fingers around him.

He sucked in a breath.

She immediately loosened her grip. "Did I hurt you?"

"Oh, yeah," he said. "But in the very best way."

She stroked his rigid length, slowly, from base to tip, then back again, and watched as his eyes darkened and a muscle in his jaw flexed as he clenched his teeth together. She stroked him again, and he caught her wrist as his breath shuddered out between his lips.

"I can't take much more of that," he warned.

"Then take me," she suggested. "I want you inside me."

"I want to be inside you," he assured her, but he lowered his head to nibble on her earlobe, kiss her throat.

"So why aren't you there?"

"Because it's been a while for me," he admitted. "And I want to make sure that it's good for you."

"It's been a while for me, too," she told him. "And I don't want to wait another minute to have you inside me."

"In that case, give me fifty-five seconds," he suggested.

"What?"

"It's less than a minute," he pointed out, as his hands leisurely traced her curves.

He continued the exploration with his mouth, kissing her breasts, her belly. He parted the soft folds of flesh at the apex of her thighs, opening her to him. Then he lowered his head and touched the sensitive nub at her center with his tongue, a slow, deliberate lick that made everything inside her tighten in glorious anticipation.

"Bailey...you don't have to—"

"Shh," he whispered against her slick flesh. "I've only got another forty seconds."

She might have smiled at that, but his mouth was already on her again, licking and nibbling, tasting and teasing. Instead, she let her head fall back against the pillow, biting down on her bottom lip to prevent herself from crying out with shock and pleasure.

She tried to hold it together. She didn't want to come apart like this. She wanted to wait until he was inside her.

Her fingers curled, fisting the cover beneath her, and she closed her eyes and tried to count down the last thirty seconds. But the numbers blurred together in her mind, as the desires and demands of her body shoved aside everything else.

"Isn't—" her breath hitched "—your time up?"

"Not just yet," he said, and continued his intimate exploration.

She couldn't fight the onslaught of sensations any longer. The tension inside her had built to a breaking point, and she shattered into a million pieces.

When her body finally stopped shuddering with aftershocks, he sheathed himself with a condom and rose up over her, then buried himself inside her.

She gasped as he filled her. Deeply. Completely.

She braced her heels on the mattress and lifted her hips, taking him even deeper, drawing a low groan of satisfaction from his throat as her muscles clenched around him.

He began to move, slowly at first, a steady rhythm that stroked deep inside her. Then faster, harder, deeper. Her hips rose to meet him and her fingernails scraped down his back as he drove them both to the pinnacle of pleasure—and beyond.

Bailey had barely managed to catch his breath when he heard Marvin's plaintive whimper through the bedroom door.

"Does he need to go out?" he asked, mumbling the question into Serena's hair.

"He has a doggy door," she reminded him.

"So why is he whining?"

"He was probably a little confused by the noises we were making," she admitted.

"You mean the noises *you* were making," he teased.

"I'm gonna plead the Fifth on that one."

He turned his head to nibble on her ear. "You were pleading something very different twenty minutes ago."

She lifted a hand to shove at his shoulder, but she didn't put much force behind the motion. "A gentleman should never embarrass a lady."

"I'm not a gentleman, I'm a cowboy," he told her.

"Well, cowboys have a code, too," she pointed out.

"Uh-huh," he agreed. "A cowboy must never shoot first, hit a smaller man or leave a woman unsatisfied."

She choked on a laugh. "I think you made that last part up."

"But did I honor the code?"

"You know you honored the code."

"Good." He lifted his head to brush his lips over hers. "Because you totally rocked my world, too."

"Yeah?"

"Oh, yeah," he confirmed.

She smiled at that. "I'm glad I walked over to the community center tonight."

He kissed her again, softly, sweetly. "I'm glad you invited me up for cocoa and cookies."

"We never had the cocoa and cookies."

"I know." Another kiss, longer, lingering. "And I'm thinking we should not have cocoa and cookies again."

"Right now?"

"Right now," he agreed.

Bailey had known that sex with Serena would be good, and he hadn't been exaggerating when he'd told her that she'd rocked his world. Of course, she was the first woman he'd been with since he'd ended his marriage, so he suspected that the extended period of celibacy had something to do with the intensity of the experience.

Except that the second time with Serena had been even better than the first. And the third had exceeded all his expectations yet again. And even after three rounds of lovemaking, his desire for her had not abated in the least.

It was that realization that caused the first hint of panic to set in. His subconscious reference to their physical joining as *lovemaking* only exacerbated it.

He wasn't in love with Serena.

He wasn't foolish enough to go down that path again, especially not with someone he'd only known a few weeks.

Sure, she was an amazing woman. Beautiful. Smart. Sexy. Passionate. Compassionate. Resilient. Caring. He could go on and on enumerating her many wonderful qualities—qualities that proved she was too good for him.

And yet, by some stroke of luck, she'd chosen to be with him. And he was selfish enough to take whatever she was willing to give, for as long as she was willing to give it.

He fell asleep with her head nestled against his shoulder—and woke up with what felt like a ten-pound weight on his chest.

Turned out it was a ten-pound cat.

"I thought you said the animals don't sleep in your bed," he remarked, when Serena returned to the bedroom from the adjoining en suite bath.

"They don't," she confirmed.

"Well, don't look now, but there's a cat on my chest."

"A wide-awake cat who wants her breakfast."

"She's not the only one," he said. Then he looked at Molly and, utilizing the same command that Serena had used so effectively with Marvin the night before, said, "Off."

The cat just stared at him, those pale green eyes unblinking.

He pointed to the floor and tried again. "Off."

Molly continued to stare at him.

"Your cat doesn't listen very well."

"She's a cat," Serena said, sounding amused.

"I can practically hear the thoughts going through her head." Then he changed the tone and pitch of his voice to recite those imagined thoughts. "I'll move my tail when I feel like moving my tail."

Serena laughed as she tied the belt of her robe around her waist. "I admit that I talk to my animals, but I don't pretend they talk back."

"Look at her and tell me that's not what she's thinking," he demanded.

She tilted her head to look at the cat. "That's not what she's thinking."

"Then what's she thinking?" he wanted to know.

"She's hoping that Santa will leave a little catnip in her stocking this year."

"Catnip, huh?"

Serena headed toward the door. "Come on, Molly."

And the damn cat followed her.

Shaking his head, Bailey pushed back the covers and climbed out of bed.

"Do I smell coffee?" he asked, when he joined her in the kitchen after he'd showered and dressed again in last night's clothes.

She handed him a mug filled with the hot fragrant brew. "What would you like for breakfast?"

"You don't have to cook for me," he said. "Or is this about balancing those scales you're so worried about?"

She laughed softly. "It's about the fact that I'm hungry and I thought you might be, too."

"I am," he confirmed.

"Eggs okay?"

"Eggs are always okay."

"Bacon?"

He nodded emphatically. "The only thing I like more than eggs."

They cooked breakfast together and ate breakfast together, and it was all very nice and domestic. And maybe it did make Serena wish she had someone with whom to share not just a single morning but the rest of her life. And maybe, if she let herself, she could imagine Bailey being that someone.

But she didn't let herself because she knew that one night did not a relationship make. She was hopeful, however, that one night might lead to two, and maybe more.

She'd just gotten up from the table for a coffee refill when the landline phone rang. A glance at the display made her pause.

"Are you going to answer that?" Bailey asked

when the phone rang again and she only continued to stare at it.

"I don't know who it is," she confessed, carrying the coffeepot to the table to top up his mug. "The area code is Arizona, which is where my grandmother lives, but the number isn't familiar."

So she let the machine answer. And because she had an old-fashioned answering machine hooked up to her landline, the message transmitted clearly through the speaker.

"Hi, Rena, it's Grams. I know you said you'd call next week when I talked to you last week, but, well, I'm not actually home right now." Then her voice dropped to a loud whisper. "I'm at George's place."

Bailey's brows lifted.

"We had the best time last night," Grams continued, and then she giggled. "And this morning."

Serena buried her face in her hands.

"Honestly, the therapeutic effects of orgasm cannot be overrated, and I know you're under a lot of stress, which is why you need to grab hold of that Stockton boy and—"

She leaped from her chair and snatched up the receiver, cutting off the recording.

"Grams, hi." She turned her back to Bailey, so that he wouldn't see that her cheeks were flaming. "I, uh, just got out of the shower."

Which wasn't technically the truth, since she'd showered when she woke up, but it wasn't exactly a lie, either.

"Do you have one of those massaging shower heads?" her grandmother asked. "I'm not saying they can replace a man's touch, but desperate times and all that."

Serena groaned inwardly. "So…tell me what's going on in your life," she said, desperate to change the subject.

For the next several minutes, her grandmother proceeded to do precisely that—in great and unnecessary detail—while Serena silently prayed that the ground would open up and swallow her. But of course that didn't happen.

"Just remember your own last rule," Serena said, when Grams paused to take a breath.

"I remember all my rules," her grandmother assured her.

"But do you follow them?"

"Oh, I've gotta run," Grams said. "George is signaling that breakfast is ready."

And before Serena could reply, she'd disconnected.

"That was your grandmother, huh?" Bailey said, amusement evident in his tone.

"That was my grandmother," she confirmed.

"And 'that Stockton boy'...that would be me?"

"So much for hoping you might pretend you hadn't heard that part," she muttered.

"Sorry," he said, not sounding sorry at all.

"But now I'm wondering what you told your grandmother about me."

"Nothing," she immediately and emphatically replied.

"And yet, she apparently wants you to grab hold of me and… What exactly was it she suggested you should do?"

"You're enjoying this a little too much."

"Not as much as I enjoyed last night," he assured her. "But that phone call certainly added something to the morning after."

"Can you please just forget about the phone call?"

"Okay," he agreed. "But tell me about your grandmother."

"What do you want to know?" she asked warily.

"It's obvious the two of you are close."

"I lived with her growing up," Serena reminded him.

"And has she always offered such interesting advice?"

She nodded. "Grams has often been exasperating and opinionated, but she loves wholeheartedly and unconditionally. She also had some pretty strict rules for anyone living under her roof."

"Like what?"

She ticked them off on her fingers as she recited: "Tell where I'm going and who I'm going with. Call when I get there. Be home by midnight. Never leave a drink unattended. Never drink and drive. Never share naked pictures. And never have sex without a condom."

"Those sound like some pretty smart and savvy rules," he remarked.

"Grams is a pretty smart and savvy lady."

"So is her granddaughter," he said.

"You think so?"

"Well, she gave me some pretty good advice."

"What advice was that?" she wondered aloud.

"About talking to Emily," he confided.

"You called her?"

He nodded. "I did."

"Was she surprised to hear from you?"

"Yeah, she was surprised to hear from me. And then she shared some surprising news."

"What was that?"

"She got married again. Six months ago."

"That's big news," Serena noted.

"And the even bigger news—she's pregnant."

"Wow."

He nodded again.

"How do you feel about that?" she asked him.

"It has nothing to do with me."

"Your ex-wife is expecting a baby with her new husband—you have to feel something."

"I'm happy for her," he said. "Really. And… relieved."

"Why relieved?" she asked, curious.

"Because there was part of me that wondered if I'd ruined her life."

"Because you divorced her?"

He shook his head. "Because I married her."

"You loved her," she reminded him.

"Or thought I did, anyway," he acknowledged. "But in retrospect, I think my decision to marry Emily was also an attempt—and not a very successful one—to take back control of my life."

"What do you mean?"

"The night my parents were killed…in addition to the grief and the guilt, I felt such an overwhelming sense of helplessness. They were gone, and there was absolutely nothing I could do to change what had happened, to fill the empty space in all of our lives.

"And then our grandparents told us there was no way that they could take in seven kids, so my two brothers and I were essentially on our own. We had no choice about that, but we chose to leave Rust Creek Falls and make our own lives. Yeah, it was a hollow victory, but we needed to feel like we had control over something.

"Everywhere I went after that, every job I took, every decision I made, was an effort to prove to myself that I was in charge of my own destiny. Then I met Emily, and I decided that I wanted to get married. But was I motivated by my feelings for her or a desperate desire to be part of a family again?"

He shrugged, as if he still wasn't certain of the answer to that question. "And does it really matter? Because I never managed to fit in with her family. I never got what I wanted. My fault, I know. Because I never really tried. Because it didn't take me long to realize that I didn't want to be part of *a* family again, I wanted *my* family back. And that was never going to happen."

He was silent for a minute, no doubt pondering those revelations. "But the point of all of that is that you were right," he continued.

"There were too many things left unsaid, and saying them will, I think, help both of us put that chapter of our lives behind us."

"I'm glad," she said sincerely.

He finished his coffee and carried his empty plate and mug to the kitchen. Setting the dishes on the counter, he pulled his cell phone out of his pocket and sighed. "Four text messages from Luke in the past hour."

"Is something wrong?" she asked, immediately concerned.

"Nah, he's just nagging me for not being there for morning chores."

"My fault," Serena realized. "Sorry."

He smiled. "I'm not." He kissed her then, softly, sweetly. "But I do have to go."

She nodded. "I know."

"I had a really good time last night."

"Me, too."

And though he'd said he had to go, he didn't

move. "I'm not sure what else to say here," he confessed.

"You don't have to say anything else," she told him.

"I want to say something else."

"What do you want to say?"

"Well, I'd like to ask if I can see you again tonight, but I don't want you to think that I'm making any assumptions…or have any expectations…that we're going to do what we did last night. Again, I mean."

She took a moment to untangle his words. "So you're saying that last night was a one-night stand?"

"No," he immediately replied. "I mean, I hope not."

"That's good," she said. "Because I hope not, too."

"So…can I see you tonight?"

"I'll be decorating my Christmas tree tonight."

"I was surprised that you didn't have one yet," he admitted.

"Me and Grams always went to get one on December 16, so I carry on that tradition," she told him.

"Where do you go?"

"Just over to the tree lot in town."

"I've got a better idea," he suggested.

"What's your better idea?" she asked warily.

"Come to Sunshine Farm with me now and we'll cut one down together and bring it back here."

"You're already late for morning chores," she reminded him.

"They'll be done before I get back."

"And you figure that your brother will be less likely to yell at you if I'm there?" she guessed.

"Do you want to hassle me or get a Christmas tree?"

She gave him a cheeky smile. "Both. But

I guess I need to put some clothes on for the latter."

He gave her a playful pat on the butt. "Be quick."

Chapter Twelve

"Are you still going to pretend that there's nothing going on between you and Serena Langley?" Dan asked Bailey.

It was Monday afternoon and the brothers had all been recruited to repair a section of downed fence at Sunshine Farm. The repair hadn't taken as long as they'd anticipated, and they were back at the barn now, attempting to warm their frozen hands with hot coffee.

"Why do you think I'm pretending?" he asked, not really denying the fact so much as wanting to know what his brother knew—or thought he did.

"Because your truck was parked outside her apartment overnight," Dan noted.

"Saturday *and* Sunday," Jamie chimed in.

"Only one of the things I forgot that I hate about small towns," Bailey grumbled.

"So what's the status of the relationship?" Luke asked.

"I don't know that I'd call it a relationship," he hedged.

"You're spending your nights in her bed," Dan said again.

"Two nights." So far. "And even in a small town, I don't think that's illegal."

"In a small town, people talk," Jamie reminded him. "And Serena's not that kind of girl."

Bailey felt a twinge of uneasiness—and not his first—as he silently acknowledged the truth of his brother's claim. Of course, he hadn't thought about the potential repercussions for her reputation when he'd accepted the invitation to go up to her apartment after the Presents for Patriots event Saturday night. He hadn't thought about anything but how much he wanted to be with her.

On the other hand, it's not as if he had a reputation for bed-hopping in town. In fact, he didn't have a reputation for much of anything, except being one of *those Stockton boys* who had returned to Rust Creek Falls after so many years away. And in the twelve months that he'd been back, Serena was the first woman he'd been with. In fact, she was the first woman he'd been with since his ex-wife—not that he had any intention of admitting as much to his brothers.

"I know you probably think this is none of our business," Luke began.

"Bingo," Bailey said.

"But it is," Dan insisted. "Not just because

you're our brother, but because Serena is a friend—a good friend—of Annie's."

"I'm aware of that," he assured his brothers. "I'm also aware that she's an adult capable of making her own decisions."

Dan held up his hands in a universal gesture of surrender. "I'm not suggesting otherwise."

"Then this conversation is over," Bailey said, looking at each of his brothers in turn.

They exchanged glances, shrugs.

"Just…be careful," Luke urged.

"I always am," he said.

But their words and warnings continued to niggle at the back of his mind throughout the rest of the day. And even when he met Serena after work, as they'd planned, to take a reluctant Marvin for a walk, followed by dinner together again.

So maybe it wasn't surprising that Serena sensed his preoccupation. Or maybe he didn't do a very good job hiding it, because when she took his hand to lead him into the living room after the dishes had been cleared up, he balked.

"What's wrong?" she asked.

"I'm wondering if I should go," he admitted.

"Oh." She immediately released his hand. "If that's what you want."

"It's not," he assured her.

"Then why are you wondering about it?"

"Because people are already talking about the fact that my truck was parked outside your apartment last night," he said. "And the night before."

"Really?" She seemed surprised by this revelation—then surprised him by smiling again. "Good."

"Why is that good?"

"Because I've always been a good girl, never giving anyone reason to speculate or gossip."

"Well, they're speculating now," he told her.

"Grams will be so proud."

"Please tell me you're not going to tell your grandmother."

"I won't have to. She'll most likely hear it from Melba Strickland—if she hasn't already."

He winced at the thought. "And then she'll wonder, along with everyone else, what a nice girl like Serena Langley is doing with an aimless boy like Bailey Stockton?"

She lifted her arms and linked her hands behind his neck, her fingertips playing with the hair that curled over the collar of his shirt. "I don't think you're aimless," she said. "You're just taking some time to figure things out."

"So what are you doing with me?" he asked her.

"I know what I want to do." She rose up onto her toes to whisper her idea in his ear.

"Your wish is my command," he said, and scooped her into his arms to carry her to the bedroom.

* * *

After that first night with Bailey, Serena knew that she was well on her way to falling in love with him. When he'd invited her to cut down a Christmas tree at Sunshine Farm, where he'd undoubtedly participated in the same ritual with his parents and siblings for the first twenty years of his life, she felt the first glimmer of hope that maybe he was starting to feel the same way.

But she didn't want to get too far ahead of herself, because she knew that he'd put shields up around his badly damaged heart, and that he might never let them down enough to fall in love again. In the meantime, she tried to enjoy just being with him and making new memories with him as they participated in all the usual holiday rituals.

Unfortunately, she couldn't spend every minute of every day with him, because they both had jobs and responsibilities. In fact, she was clipping the nails of a Great Dane Wednesday afternoon when a knock sounded on the door, then Bailey stepped into the exam room.

"Annie said it was okay for me to come in," he explained.

"Sure," she agreed. "Tiny is always happy to meet new people." The Great Dane's tail thumped noisily against the surface of the metal table, but otherwise, the animal didn't move as she continued to work.

Bailey made a show of looking around the room. "Where's Tiny?"

She smiled. "*This* is Tiny."

"I doubt that animal was ever tiny, even as a puppy," he remarked.

"Norma Wilson has a fondness for irony," Serena explained. "Her other dog is a Chihuahua named Monster." She clipped the last nail. "All done."

Tiny nimbly hopped down off the table. Standing, his head was level with Serena's midriff. Then he dropped to his butt on the floor, sitting patiently, expectantly.

She retrieved a treat from the pocket of her lab coat and fed it to him. "Good boy," she said, and rubbed the top of his head.

"Do I get a treat?" Bailey asked.

She offered him a doggy cookie.

He lowered his head and kissed her instead.

"That's what I wanted," he told her.

"That was nice," she agreed. "But I suspect you didn't come into town just for a kiss."

"No," he agreed. "Not that one of your kisses wouldn't make the trip worthwhile, but Luke asked me to pick up some stuff at the feed store. And since I was here, I thought I'd check in to see if you wanted to reschedule the dinner and a movie that we missed last week. How's Friday night?"

"Actually, I already have plans for Friday night," she confided.

"Oh." He frowned. "What kind of plans?"

"The Candlelight Walk."

He looked at her blankly.

"Maybe you weren't back in town yet when it happened last year," she acknowledged. "It's exactly what the name implies—residents carry lit candles in a processional down Main Street."

"Yeah, I guess I missed that," he said.

"You don't sound too sorry," she noted.

He shrugged. "You know all that Christmassy stuff isn't really my thing."

"Which is why I didn't ask you to go with me."

"But if my only options are a Candlelight Walk with you or spending Friday night alone... Well, there's no contest."

"Really? You want to go with me?"

"I really want to go with you," he said.

She was used to feeling butterflies in her tummy.

The first time she'd ever met Bailey Stockton, a brief and impromptu introduction at the clinic one day when he'd stopped by to see Annie, Serena had felt flutters in her belly. And again, a few months later, when she'd crossed paths with him at Crawford's. And of course, the day that they'd played Santa and Mrs. Claus at the community center.

They'd spent a lot of time together since then, and yet, all it took was a look, a smile or a touch to have those butterflies swooping and spinning again.

As she got ready for the Candlelight Walk, she felt as if those familiar butterflies had multiplied tenfold—and then OD'd on caffeine. Because Serena knew that showing up at tonight's event with Bailey would make a statement about their relationship that would carry as much weight as a headline in the *Gazette*.

Even as she added a spritz of her favorite perfume, she wondered if this was a bad idea. If she was making their relationship into more than it really was. When she was with him, she was usually having too much fun to worry that she might be the only one emotionally invested in the relationship. It was only when she was on her own, with the holidays looming, that the doubts and insecurities raised their ugly heads.

Because each day that passed was a day closer to December 25, and Bailey had said nothing about his plans for Christmas—or asked about hers.

Not that she had any plans. While many residents of Rust Creek Falls were busy running here or there to spend time with family or friends, Serena was accustomed to being on her own with her pets. And that was okay. It was her own tradition—a day of quiet reflection and counting her blessings.

It was another tradition to spend the day after Christmas with her mother, *if* Amanda felt up to it. But her mother was spending the holidays with Mark this year, and although they were keeping their celebrations low-key, they'd invited Serena to join them. Of course, she'd declined. Not only because she didn't want to intrude on their first Christmas together, but because she was—perhaps foolishly—optimistic that she might be celebrating her own first Christmas with Bailey.

But she had accepted an invitation to Mark's house for lunch on Sunday, just two days before Christmas, and she'd ordered a Dutch apple pie—her mother's favorite—from Daisy's as her contribution to the meal. She'd told Bailey of her plans, emphasizing the fact that she didn't celebrate Christmas Day with her mom, but he hadn't taken the hint.

Of course, he'd only reunited with his family the previous year, so it was understandable that they'd be the focus of his plans. It was also possible that he planned to invite her to celebrate with him but hadn't yet done so.

Maybe tonight, she thought—fingers crossed—

as she retrieved her hat and mittens from the closet. Then she reached for her boots, and Marvin immediately went to hide.

She laughed, then winced a little as she tightened the lace of her right boot. She'd had a little mishap at the clinic the day before and twisted her ankle. Although she'd iced and wrapped the joint, it was still a little sore—but not sore enough to keep her from participating in one of her favorite holiday events.

She'd just finished buttoning her coat when Bailey knocked at the door. He kissed her lightly, then looked at the floor by her feet. "Where's Marvin?"

"Hiding," she said.

"Why?"

"Because these are my *w-a-l-k-i-n-g* boots," she explained. "And not even the promise of a belly rub would entice him out for a second *w-a-l-k* in one day."

"That dog has issues," he told her.

"And his exercise phobia is only the tip of the iceberg," she admitted, as she closed and locked the door behind her. "He's also afraid of horses, cows and pigs."

"You're kidding."

"Nope." She shook her head as she descended the stairs beside him, trying not to put her full weight on her right foot. "One day when we were out, there were a couple of young girls riding horses on a trail, and he darted between my legs and would not move."

"Then that might be another reason he's hiding," Bailey suggested, as he led her around to the front of the building.

She halted in midstep. "What's this?"

"What does it look like?"

"It looks like a horse-drawn sleigh."

"Got it in one," he told her. "More specifically, it's a two-seat Albany sleigh."

And it was gorgeous, with gleaming bronze

accents and tufted velvet seats and ribbon-wrapped pine boughs adding a festive touch.

"*Where* did you get it?" she asked him now.

"I borrowed it from Dallas Traub. And Trina—" he gestured to the gorgeous horse harnessed to the sleigh "—from his stables."

"Okay," she said. "But *why* did you borrow a horse-drawn sleigh for the Candlelight *Walk*?"

"Because Annie told me that you sprained your ankle at work—which you didn't mention to me," he said pointedly.

"Because it's fine," she assured him.

He just lifted a brow.

"And it's wrapped."

"But I don't imagine it will feel very good tomorrow if you're on it all night tonight."

"Probably not," she acknowledged. "But I didn't want to miss the walk."

"And now you don't have to," he said, taking her hand to help her climb into the seat.

"This is so…thoughtful."

"And romantic?" he suggested.

"Unbelievably romantic," she assured him.

And it was.

The walk started at the high end of Main Street, where volunteers from the city council handed out lighted candles in tall glass jars. Bailey left her in the sleigh while he went to get a candle for her, then they took their position at the rear of the crowd. Of course, night fell early in December, but the flicker of so many candles created a beautiful golden glow as the processional made its way slowly toward the park, where the bonfire would be lit.

Bailey held the reins in one gloved hand and Serena's free hand with his other.

"People are going to talk," she warned.

"People are already talking," he reminded her.

"And you just added fresh fuel to the fire."

"With this?" he scoffed, lifting their joined hands. "I doubt it. But maybe—" he tipped her chin up and brushed his lips over hers "—that will do the trick."

"If the trick is making me want to skip the bonfire and take you home to have my way with you, then yes."

"Participating in tonight's festivities was *your* idea," he reminded her.

"So it was," she confirmed.

And she was glad he'd agreed to come. Not only because he'd so thoughtfully provided transportation that allowed her to rest her sore ankle, but because she always enjoyed being with him.

At the end of the route, after the bonfire had been lit, eliciting gasps and cheers from the crowd, they caught sight of his brother Jamie with Fallon and the triplets, Henry, Jared and Katie.

The kids were excited to see "ho-zees," and after checking with Serena first, Bailey offered the reins to his brother so that he and his wife could take their kids for a little ride.

While they were gone, Bailey and Serena mingled with the crowd. And it was a crowd. The O'Reillys were in attendance en masse: Paddy and Maureen, their sons, Ronan and Keegan, and their daughters, Fallon, Fiona and Brenna, along with their respective partners. There were several representatives of each of the Crawford and Traub families, and even more Daltons.

They stopped to chat for a minute with Old Gene and Melba Strickland, the latter asking about Serena's grandmother. And though Serena was tempted to point out that Melba probably talked to Janet Carswell more than her granddaughter did, she managed to bite back the cheeky retort and simply assure the older woman that Janet was doing well.

Shortly after that, Jamie and Fallon returned and they traded places again, then Bailey directed Trina to take them back to Serena's place.

"Tonight was…amazing," Serena said, after he'd carried her up the stairs to her back door.

"I'm glad you had a good time."

"I suppose you have to get the horse and sleigh back to the Triple T," she said, naming the Traub ranch where Dallas and Nina lived with their four children.

"I do," Bailey confirmed.

"Do you want to come back here after you've done that?" she asked him.

He tightened his arms around her. "What horse and sleigh?"

She laughed softly. "I'm flattered. I know you wouldn't really neglect Trina after she dutifully escorted us around town all night, but I'm flattered."

"I'll be back as soon as I can," he promised.

"I'll be here," she assured him.

He kept his promise.

And when he made love to her that night, it was beautiful and magical and Serena finally acknowledged a truth she'd been trying to deny: she was in love with Bailey Stockton.

The realization filled her heart with joy—and her belly with trepidation. Because she knew that Bailey wasn't looking for a serious relationship. He'd been honest about that from the very beginning. But she'd fallen in love with him anyway.

She'd never felt like this before, and she was torn between wanting to tell him and worrying that if she did, the confession of her feelings would act as a wedge rather than a bridge between them. So for now, she resolved to keep the words to herself.

But as their bodies merged together in the darkness of the night, she knew that the truth and depth of her feelings were evident in every touch of her lips, pass of her hands and press of her body.

* * *

"You know, the first pie I ever made for Luke was an apple," Eva said conversationally, as she boxed up the dessert Serena had ordered.

"Proving that the way to a man's heart is through his stomach?" Serena guessed.

"Well, I can't argue with the results." The other woman grinned as she fluttered the fingers of her left hand, where a glittery diamond nestled against the wedding band on the third finger.

Serena smiled back as she passed her money across the counter.

"So are you going to tell me what this pie is for?" Eva prompted. "Or are you going to make me guess?"

"I'm going to lunch at my mother's boyfriend's house." It felt strange to say those words—*mother's boyfriend*—but Amanda and Mark seemed to have clearly defined their relationship, while Serena and Bailey had not.

"I would have guessed wrong," the baker said. "Is Bailey going with you?"

Serena shook her head. "No."

"Why not?"

"Because I didn't invite him."

"Why not?" Eva asked again.

"Because I'm not even sure *I* want to go," Serena admitted. "I certainly wouldn't drag anyone else into the center of my family drama."

"Every family has drama," Eva assured her. "And nothing shines twinkling lights on it like the holidays."

"Isn't that the truth?" she agreed.

"So...what are your plans for Christmas Eve?"

"Oh, the usual," Serena said, deliberately vague.

"What's the usual?"

"Hanging out with Marvin, Molly and Max," she confided.

The other woman's eyes narrowed. "Isn't Marvin your dog?"

Serena nodded. "My dog, my cat and my bunny."

"You don't spend Christmas Eve with your mom?"

"That would be too much drama even for me."

"In that case, you should come out to Sunshine Farm," Eva said.

"Oh." Serena was taken aback by the other woman's impulsive offer—and undeniably touched by the invitation. "Thanks, but I wouldn't want to intrude on your family celebrations."

"Don't be silly," the baker chided. "Everyone will be happy to see you."

"I don't know," she hedged. "Bailey hasn't said anything to me about his plans for the holidays." He certainly hadn't given any indication that he wanted to spend them with her.

"Because he's a man. He doesn't know how to make plans any more than twenty-four hours in advance of an event."

Serena smiled, but she wasn't convinced—especially since Christmas Eve was less than twenty-four hours away.

"Say you'll come," Eva urged. "It will be a lot more fun than hanging out with Marvin, Molly and Matt."

"Max," she corrected automatically. "And our holiday snuggles are something of a tradition."

"But I bet you'd rather snuggle with Bailey," his sister-in-law teased.

Serena couldn't deny it.

And Eva, confident that she'd made another sale, said, "Dinner will be on the table at six."

Two days before Christmas, Bailey wrapped the last of his gifts—this one for Serena.

It wasn't anything fancy or expensive, just a simple eight-by-ten enlargement of a photo of the animals that he'd snapped with his cell phone one day when he was at her apartment. In the picture, Marvin was sprawled out on his belly—his back end on his pillow, his shoulders and head on the floor; Max was stretched out beside him but facing the opposite direction; and Molly was curled up with her face right beside Max's and one paw on his back. The candid shot attested to the camaraderie and affection between the animals, and he was confident Serena would love it.

He had yet to decide how and when he was going to give it to her. Because holding hands and stealing kisses in public was one thing, while sharing a major holiday took a relationship to the next level, and he wasn't sure they were ready to go there—or that they ever would be.

He always had a great time with Serena, and he thought of her often when they were apart, but that didn't mean he was ready to commit to a capital-*R* relationship. And spending Christmas together definitely implied Relationship, which was why he'd decided to fly solo over the holidays.

And why he was taken aback when Luke's wife told him what she'd done.

Chapter Thirteen

"You did what?" Bailey said, certain he must have misunderstood or misinterpreted Eva's words.

"I invited Serena to come over on Christmas Eve," she repeated.

"Why?" he demanded to know.

She frowned, obviously not having anticipated his less-than-enthusiastic response to her announcement. "Because she came in to Daisy's and when I asked about her plans for the holidays, she admitted that—aside from hanging out at home with her pets—she didn't have any."

"She loves hanging out at home with her pets," he informed his sister-in-law. "It's kind of her thing."

"And because I thought you'd want her to be here," Eva added.

"You should have asked me before you asked her," he grumbled.

Her expression shifted from bafflement to concern. "Do you not want her here?"

"I just don't want her to think an invitation to spend Christmas Eve with my family means anything more than that."

"Serena doesn't strike me as the type of woman who would assume a casual invitation from her boyfriend's sister-in-law is a green light to start planning the seating chart for your wedding," she said dryly.

"I'm not her boyfriend," he said through gritted teeth.

"So what are you?" she challenged. "Just a guy who's bouncing on her bed for as long as it suits his purposes?"

That was all he'd wanted, but to hear his brother's wife put it in such blunt terms sounded harsh. And untrue.

"Why does everyone want to put a label on our relationship?" Because as much as he hadn't wanted a relationship, he couldn't deny that he was in one.

He cared about Serena. He enjoyed being with her. And yes, he enjoyed sex with her. But even he couldn't deny that their relationship was about more than sex. He liked talking to her, he appreciated the comfortable silences they shared, he even liked hanging out with her pets. Although Marvin was undeniably his favorite, he had no issues with Max and felt reasonably confident that he'd reached a détente with Molly.

But he wasn't ready for another Relationship.

Or maybe he didn't trust himself not to mess up with Serena the way he'd messed up his marriage.

"Do you want me to uninvite her?" Eva asked him now.

"Is there any possible way to do that without an incredible amount of awkwardness?" he wondered aloud.

"Probably not," she admitted. "But I'd rather have an awkward conversation with Serena today than have her feel uncomfortable or unwelcome tomorrow."

"Don't bother," he said. "It's fine."

But Serena was right. Saying "it's fine" didn't make it so, and Bailey decided to go for a drive to clear his head.

Although he had no destination in mind when he set out, he wasn't really surprised when he found his truck slowing down as he approached the cemetery.

His heart was pounding hard against his ribs

and his palms were clammy as he shifted into Park and turned off the ignition. He hadn't been here since that awful day his parents were put in the ground, and he was immediately swamped by a wave of memories and emotions. He pushed open the door and stepped out into the cold.

Someone had put an evergreen wreath decorated with holly berries and pinecones on an easel in the ground beside the headstone. Bella, he guessed. It was the type of thing she would think to do. He knew that she visited the cemetery regularly, and throughout the summer tended to the flowers she planted in the spring.

He took a couple steps forward and dropped to his knees in the snow, his watery gaze unable to focus on the names and dates etched in the stone. It didn't matter—the details were forever etched in his mind. The regrets forever heavy in his heart.

"I've screwed everything up," Bailey said,

somehow managing to force the words through his closed-up throat. "Starting with that night in the bar, thirteen years ago." He shook his head. "I was so careless, so thoughtless. So stupid."

That long ago night, he'd ignored Danny's urgings to leave because there were pretty girls to dance with and beer to drink. And yeah, he'd actually thought it was funny that his little brother was such an uptight mother hen.

I've already got one mother. I don't need another one, he'd chided his brother.

Danny's expression had darkened, but Luke had laughed—sharing the joke, the good times.

Then the sheriff's deputy had walked into the bar, and the laughter had stopped.

"It was my fault," Bailey confessed to his parents as he stared at the headstone. "But they don't blame me. I don't know how or why, but Bella, Jamie, Dana…even Luke and Danny… don't blame me for what happened that night.

But I know the truth. It was my fault. Serena thinks I'm still punishing myself. That I won't let myself be happy because I don't believe I deserve to be happy.

"She might be right," he acknowledged. "I never told Emily about that night, because I was afraid she'd look at me differently. At least, that was the justification I gave to myself. But maybe I wasn't ready to let go of any of my guilt and grief enough to share it."

It was a possibility he hadn't considered until right now. A truth that suddenly seemed unassailable.

"But somehow, I found myself telling Serena everything. Maybe because she's had to overcome devastating losses of her own. And yet, despite that, she is one of the most optimistic people I've ever met. Determined to find happiness in every day—and adding joy to mine whenever I'm with her.

"I really wish you could have met her—and

that she'd had the chance to know you. She really is amazing. Beautiful and smart. Sexy and sweet." His smile was wry. "And undoubtedly too good for me."

Of course, there was no response to his monologue. But when Bailey finally rose to his feet again, his heart felt lighter. And for the first time in a long time, he felt hopeful about his future and willing to not just appreciate but embrace the joy that Serena brought to his life.

For a dozen years, Bailey hadn't thought he had any reason to celebrate the holidays. Last year, his first back in Rust Creek Falls after twelve away, he'd felt awkward and uncomfortable, like an imposter in his sister's home. Not that Bella had done or said anything to make him feel less than welcome. Just the opposite, in fact. She'd gone out of her way for him, even ensuring there were presents with his name on them under the tree Christmas morning.

But this year, being with his siblings again, along with their significant others and kids, he truly felt as if he was where he belonged. Even Dana had made the trip from Oregon— with the blessing of her adoptive parents—to spend the holiday with her brothers and sister.

Of course, the entire family wasn't there, but those who gathered together found pleasure in their renewed and strengthened childhood bonds and remembered those who weren't with them at Sunshine Farm. They all hoped that Liza would also be brought back into the fold someday, but for now, Bailey focused on being grateful for what he had—including the beautiful woman by his side.

"So tell me how you and Bailey met," Dana said to Serena.

"Well, I actually met him several months ago at the vet clinic where I work with Annie," she said. "But I didn't really get to know him until Dan went down with the flu. Bailey had to fill in for him playing Santa, and I did the same for Annie as Mrs. Claus, so she could take care of her sick husband."

"I guess it's lucky for both of you that Dan got the flu," Dana remarked.

Janie, only hearing the last part of her aunt's remark as she came into the living room from the kitchen, stopped in the entrance and looked worriedly toward the sofa, where her parents were seated. "Dad's got the flu?"

"Not now," her mother hastened to assure her. "He's fully recuperated now."

Janie looked puzzled. "When was he sick?" she wondered aloud.

"When Uncle Bailey had to fill in as Santa at the community center," Annie said.

"And your school," Dan chimed in.

"Oh, right." Janie chuckled, remembering. "Your fake flu."

Bailey frowned. "Fake flu?"

"Yeah," his niece confirmed, apparently

oblivious to the can of worms she was opening. "Mom and Dad thought that forcing you to play Santa would help put you in the holiday spirit."

A heavy silence followed Janie's revelation, until Fallon spoke up. "Did you hear that?" she asked, though no one had heard anything. "I think the kids are starting to wake up. Janie, can you help me with them?"

"Sure," the tween agreed, always happy to lend a hand with her toddler cousins.

"I'll help, too," the triplets' father said. "Three sets of hands are always best with three kids," Jamie explained.

Bailey waited until they'd gone before he turned to Dan. "You *faked* being sick?"

"I did have a bit of a cold," Dan said defensively.

"You told me you were throwing up," Bailey reminded him. Then he turned to his brother's wife. "And you acted so concerned—going to

Daisy's to get him soup. You even had Serena fill in for you because you couldn't risk leaving your oh-so-sick husband alone." He shook his head. "And now I find out it was all just part of the act."

"Or was it a romantic setup from the beginning?" Eva mused aloud. Head over heels in love with her husband, she wished for a happy ending for everyone.

The color that filled Annie's cheeks answered the question before she spoke. "I might have asked Serena to take my place because I hoped she and Bailey would hit it off."

"And she was right," Dana pointed out, obviously trying to ease the tensions between her siblings.

Serena could tell that Bailey wasn't in a mood to be appeased. Not that she could blame him for being angry and upset by the machinations of his brother and sister-in-law. She was none too happy herself—and more than a little embarrassed—to have been so completely caught up in the plot.

"Did you have any part in this?" he asked her now.

She immediately shook her head. "Of course not," she denied, shocked that Bailey could believe such a thing.

And maybe he didn't, but he was apparently too mad to think rationally right now.

He turned to his brother again. "You always think you know what's best for everyone else, don't you? Consequences be damned." Bailey didn't raise his voice, and his words were almost more lethal because of their quiet fury. "I would have thought you'd learned your lesson about sticking your nose into other people's business thirteen years ago."

When Dan's face drained of all color, Serena realized the brothers were arguing about something more than a feigned illness.

"That's enough," Luke said to his brothers.

But Dan refused to heed the warning. "Maybe I was, in a small way, trying to make up for mistakes I made in the past," he acknowledged. "Maybe I was trying to help you find the happiness you don't think you deserve."

"Contrary to what you think, I can manage my own life," Bailey said. "I don't need anyone's interference."

He turned on Eva now, as if having finally let his emotions loose, he couldn't stop. "And I certainly don't need anyone to set me up with a date on Christmas Eve. If I'd wanted a date, I would have got one myself—but I didn't."

The implication of his pointed words was unmistakable, and Serena flinched from the verbal blow. If she'd ever had any illusions that she belonged here, with Bailey, the vehemence of his response ripped that veil away.

Another, even heavier, silence fell around the room.

"Well," Serena said, clearing her throat to speak around the lump that was sitting there. "I think it's time for me to be on my way."

"But…we haven't eaten yet," Dana pointed out.

"And I've got animals at home that need to be fed," Serena said.

No one said anything else then. No one else tried to stop her. Certainly not Bailey.

She didn't look in his direction as she made her way out of the room. And she didn't hurry, keeping her chin up and her gaze focused ahead of her as she made her escape, so that no one would guess her heart was breaking into a million jagged little pieces.

She found her boots easily enough, but there were so many coats piled onto the hooks by the door, it took her a minute to uncover hers. Of course, her efforts were further thwarted by the tears that blurred her vision.

She'd been a fool to think that they were

growing closer, maybe even building a relationship. She'd had reservations about accepting
Eva's invitation to spend Christmas Eve with
the Stocktons at Sunshine Farm, but Bailey's
sister-in-law had assured her that he would
want her there.

The silence in the living room had been broken. Voices were raised now, talking over one
another so that she couldn't make out what anyone was saying—and she was grateful for it.
Finally, she found her coat, shoved her arms
into the sleeves, stuffed her feet into her boots
and yanked open the door.

She blinked in surprise as she got a face full
of snowflakes. An hour earlier, as she'd driven
toward Sunshine Farm, she'd been enchanted
by the pretty flakes dancing harmlessly in the
sky. The wind had obviously picked up since
then and the snow was falling heavily now—
no longer appearing pretty or harmless.

Swiping at a tear that spilled onto her cheek,

she inhaled a slow, deep breath. The icy air sliced like a sharply honed blade through her lungs, but that pain didn't compare to the ache in her heart.

She unlocked her SUV and climbed in. Shoving her key into the ignition, she cranked up the defroster and turned on the wipers. The snow that had accumulated on the windshield was swept away by the blades, and she shifted into Reverse, carefully backing around the other vehicles parked in the long drive. Cars and trucks that belonged to Bailey's brothers and sisters. Proof that he was surrounded by family. Proof that he didn't need her.

He'd referred to his family, with equal parts exasperation and affection, as nosy and interfering. And what Dan and Annie had done proved his description was apt. But Serena had no doubt that his brother and sister-in-law had acted with the best of intentions, wanting him to find the same kind of happiness they'd found together.

Still, Serena could understand why he was angry, if not the intensity of his anger. Or maybe she could. The day he'd told her about his long overdue conversation with his ex-wife, he'd also told her how much he'd hated feeling as if he didn't have any control over his life after his parents were killed. So maybe it was understandable that he'd be furious about the setup, because regardless of Dan and Annie's motivations, they'd taken control of the situation away from Bailey.

She believed the feelings they had for one another were real, but she could see why the manipulation of the situation might lead Bailey to question the legitimacy of his emotions. And that was something he needed to figure out on his own—if he even wanted to. Obviously the Stockton siblings had some other issues to work through, but she had no doubt that they would do so, because no matter their differences, they were a family who cared deeply about one another.

She thought of her own family—of herself, her mother and her grandmother. Three generations of women who had been through so much—and nearly let their trials tear them apart. But even the deepest wounds eventually healed, and for the first time in a lot of years, Serena felt optimistic about her mother's recovery and the relationship they were gradually beginning to rebuild.

Amanda was with Mark today. He understood that Christmas was a particularly difficult time for her and was happy to give her whatever support she needed to make it through the holidays without falling apart—or falling back into old habits.

Serena would celebrate this year the same way she'd done last year and the one before that—with Marvin, Molly and Max. She didn't need anyone else. Certainly not some stupid man who didn't know how lucky he was to have her.

And yeah, maybe she didn't need Bailey, but she couldn't deny that she loved him.

And it hurt to know that he didn't love her back.

Fresh tears filled her eyes, spilled onto her cheeks.

She didn't lift her hands from the wheel to wipe them away, because the snow was coming really fast and heavy now, and she felt her tires slip on patches of ice beneath the fresh snow. Her mechanic had warned her that she needed new snow tires, but she'd been certain that she could get one more winter out of them. She silently pleaded not to be proved wrong now.

"The Christmas Song" was playing on the local radio station she always listened to, and when Nat King Cole finished singing, the deejay's voice came through the speaker.

"I hope everyone's enjoying their Christmas Eve—and staying off the roads. Our local law enforcement has issued the following weather warning and travel advisory—heavy snow with significant blowing and drifting is imminent or occurring. Snowfall amounts up to eighteen inches with blizzard to near-blizzard conditions likely in many areas, making travel difficult or dangerous with road closures possible.

"So if you don't have to be out and about, pour yourself a glass of eggnog and sit back with your feet up by the fire and listen to the sounds of the season. I'm here to keep you company all night long."

It was good advice, and Serena vowed to do exactly as he suggested as soon as she got home.

But first she had to get home.

A flash of something caught the corner of her eye. She eased up on the gas and turned her head just in time to see a white-tailed deer leap up out of the ditch and onto the road ahead.

She instinctively hit the brakes to avoid hitting the majestic creature, but she braked a little too hard for the conditions. Her tires slid on the slick road, and the back end of her SUV fishtailed.

She immediately tried to steer into the skid, but her efforts had little effect. The vehicle continued to spin, as if in slow motion, then slid into the ditch. Because the point of impact was at the rear, the airbag didn't deploy, but she was thrown against her seat belt and then, when the SUV abruptly listed, she smacked her head against the driver's side window.

She winced at the explosion of pain and felt a trickle of something wet sliding down the side of her face. Had the window cracked? Was it snow?

She wiped it away, then saw the back of her hand was smeared with red.

Not snow.

Blood.

Merry frickin' Christmas to me.

Chapter Fourteen

She didn't get out of the vehicle. There was no point. She could tell by the angle of the hood sticking in the air that she wasn't going to get out of the ditch without a tow cable. So she unclipped her seat belt to retrieve her purse, which had slid off the passenger seat to the floor. She winced a little, realizing that her shoulder was tender from the restraint. Thankfully, she hadn't been driving too fast, but she had no doubt she'd have plenty of bumps and bruises the next day.

She found her phone and swiped to unlock the screen. It remained blank.

Fresh tears burned her eyes. She was heart-broken, frustrated and angry. It was Christmas Eve and she just wanted to be home with Molly and Marvin and Max. Instead, she was stranded in a snowbank on the side of the road with a dead cell phone.

She never should have accepted Eva's invitation to spend Christmas Eve with the Stocktons at Sunshine Farm. She should have known that Bailey not asking her wasn't an oversight but an indication that he didn't want her there. She should have been satisfied with their friend-ship-with-benefits and not allowed herself to hope and believe the relationship could turn into anything more.

She dropped her forehead against the steer-ing wheel as hot tears spilled onto her cheeks. She wasn't really hurt—not physically. But her heart was battered, her spirit beaten down. And because it was Christmas Eve and the whole town was experiencing blizzard conditions, she estimated the chances of another motorist passing by were slim to none.

Thankfully, she kept a spare charger in her center console. She also found a travel pack of tissues there. After plugging the charger into her phone, she pulled out a couple of tissues and pressed them to her temple to stanch the flow of blood.

Squinting through the window, she saw lights in the distance. Could it be...? Was that another vehicle coming her way?

Her bruised heart gave a joyful little jump.

Maybe her luck was turning around. Maybe something was finally going to go her way today.

She used the sleeve of her coat to wipe condensation off the side window—not that it helped much. She could barely see anything through the blowing snow, but she was almost certain now that there were headlights drawing nearer.

Apparently she wasn't the only resident of Rust Creek Falls who had disregarded the travel warning. Although, in her defense, she'd been unaware of the warning until she'd left Sunshine Farm and was already on her way toward home. Not that she would have stayed, even if she'd known about the road conditions. Not after Bailey had made it clear to everyone that she wasn't wanted.

She rubbed a hand over the ache in the center of her chest. Yeah, the truth hurt, but she would get over it—and him. It might take some time, she knew, but her heart had already proven its resilience, time and again.

As the vehicle drew closer, she saw that it was a blue pickup. Like Bailey's truck.

And her bruised heart gave another little jump.

She immediately chided herself for the reaction and dismissed the possibility. It couldn't be Bailey's truck. He'd made it clear that he didn't want her at Sunshine Farm, so there was no reason to suspect that he might have followed her when she'd gone.

Of course, it was possible that he'd left the ranch for another reason, although she couldn't imagine one that would compel him to venture out in such nasty weather.

But as the truck drew nearer, she realized that it *was* Bailey's truck.

So much for thinking this was a lucky break. She already felt like a fool. The absolute last thing she needed was for the man who'd callously broken her heart to ride to her rescue. Because of course he would stop, and then he would insist on driving her home. And every mile of the journey would be excruciating painful.

If I'd wanted a date, I would have got one myself.

She winced at the echo of his words in her head.

His vehicle slowed and carefully eased over

to the side of the road behind her incapacitated SUV.

Serena swiped at the tears on her cheeks, not wanting him to know that she'd been crying. Not wanting him to think that she was crying over him.

Before she could catch her breath, her door was wrenched open from the outside and a blast of cold swept through the interior of the cab and stole her breath.

"Oh my God, Serena—what happened? Are you hurt?" He sounded genuinely concerned, maybe even a little panicked. "You're bleeding," he said, then lifted a hand to her chin and gently turned her face so that he could inspect the gash above her eye.

"I braked to avoid hitting a deer," she confided.

"Of course, you did," he said, shaking his head. "Without thinking about the potential danger to yourself."

"It was an instinct," she said, a little defensively.

"Do you need a doctor? An ambulance?"

This time she shook her head, wincing as the movement escalated the throbbing inside her skull. "I'm okay. Just…stuck. I was going to call for a tow when I saw your headlights."

"It might take a tow truck driver a while to get out here, if you can find one willing to venture out in this storm. Everyone's being advised to avoid nonessential travel."

"I heard that on the radio…while I was driving," she admitted. "But why are *you* out on the roads?"

"Because I'm an idiot," he said. "And I'm sorry."

He reached into the cab to pull her into his arms and hold her close.

Serena remained perfectly still, not sure how she was supposed to respond to this unexpected show of concern. Not willing to let herself believe that anything had changed in the short time that had passed since she left Sunshine Farm.

"I'm so sorry, Serena." He whispered the words close to her ear, his tone thick with emotion.

"Why are you sorry?" she asked cautiously.

"Because I'm an idiot," he said again, his arms still wrapped tight around her, as if he couldn't bear to let her go. "I got mad at Danny for butting in, because I'd finally started to believe that I was back in control of my life, and finding out that he'd manipulated the situation… Well, it set me off," he admitted. "But obviously I do need someone to tell me what to do, because I just seem to screw everything up otherwise."

"You don't need to apologize for your feelings," she responded stiffly.

He loosened his hold enough to draw back to look at her—or maybe so that she could see the sincerity in his eyes. "I'm not apologizing for my feelings. I'm apologizing for *denying* my feelings—and for letting you get caught in the middle of an old dispute."

She shrugged, still reluctant to let herself hope. "I shouldn't have been where I obviously wasn't wanted."

"But I *did* want you there," he insisted. "And I was afraid to admit that I wanted you there. I was afraid to admit how much I want our relationship to work, so I sabotaged it instead. Because letting you go seemed easier than letting you into my heart."

"Then…why did you follow me?"

"Because the door had barely closed behind you when I realized that you're already in my heart, and I don't ever want to let you go." He lifted his hands to frame her face. "Maybe Dan and Annie manipulated the situation, but my feelings are real. I love you, Serena, and I want to spend not just this Christmas but all Christmases for the rest of my life with you."

His declaration—so unexpected and unexpectedly perfect—brought fresh tears to her eyes.

"Don't cry, Serena. I know I hurt you, but it can't be too late. Please tell me it's not too late."

"It's not too late," she assured him. "These are happy tears."

"Do they mean that you forgive me?" he asked hopefully.

"I forgive you. And I love you, too."

His lips curved. "Yeah?"

"Yeah," she confirmed. "For now and forever."

"Will you come back to celebrate Christmas with me and my noisy, nosy family?" he asked.

"Will you do me a favor?"

"Anything," he promised.

"Give me a ride," she said. "Because my vehicle isn't going anywhere anytime soon."

* * *

So they returned to Sunshine Farm, where the rest of the Stockton family was relieved to see her—although distressed by the sight of her injury. But after Annie and Eva had finished fussing and cleaning and bandaging her wound, they all *finally* sat down to dinner.

"I've already apologized to Serena," Bailey told his siblings, after the food had been passed around and everyone had loaded up their plates. "But I want to apologize to all of you, too, for my ill-mannered outburst."

"Since you apparently came to your senses and got back your girl, I guess we can forgive you," Jamie said.

Bailey smiled as he slid an arm around Serena's shoulders. "Did you hear that? You're my girl."

"I heard," she confirmed. "And I think that's a title I can live with."

"Good. Because I don't want to live without

you." Then he glanced across the table at Dan and Annie. "And I guess I should thank both of you for introducing me to Mrs. Claus..." He paused then and turned back to Serena. "Or maybe...the future Mrs. Stockton?"

Serena stared at him, stunned. "Are you..." She let the words trail off, unwilling to complete the thought, in case she was wrong.

"I'm asking if you'll marry me, Serena."

She wasn't wrong. And with those words, her heart filled with so much happiness and love, she could barely breathe never mind respond to his question.

"Yay!" Janie immediately cheered. "There's going to be another wedding."

Henry, Jared and Katie—likely picking up on the excitement of their cousin's tone more than understanding her words—responded by clapping their hands.

"While I appreciate your enthusiastic support," Bailey said to his nieces and nephews,

"Serena hasn't yet answered my question." Then he turned his gaze back to her. "What do you say?"

"I say yes," she told him. "Definitely yes."

A quick—and decidedly relieved—grin creased his face for an instant before he kissed her.

And then everyone was cheering and applauding.

"I know it's impolite to eat and run," Jamie noted, peering out the window as the table was being cleared a long while later. "But it's really snowing out there."

"It really is," Fallon agreed. "We should get the kids bundled up and make our escape while we still can."

"*If* you still can," Eva said, looking worried.

"Why don't you spend the night here?" Luke suggested as an alternative. "After all, we have plenty of cabins."

"Because Santa Claus is coming tonight," Fallon reminded them all.

"And we're not going far," Jamie pointed out. "Not to mention that Andy and Molly would be very unhappy to be left alone overnight," he said, referring to the puppies he'd adopted out of the litter of seven that he'd rescued two years earlier.

"What about Marvin?" Bailey suddenly asked Serena. "What if his doggy door gets blocked by the snow?"

"I already called Dee," she said, referring to the neighbor who occasionally checked in on her animals when Serena had to be away for any length of time. "She'll make sure the animals have everything they need."

"Does she know to give Max his apple wedge treat? And to fluff Molly's pillow?"

"She knows," Serena assured him.

But in that moment, she knew that if she hadn't already been head over heels in love with him, Bailey's concern for the welfare of her furry companions would have made her tumble.

"So they'll be okay if you stay here with me tonight?" he prompted.

"They might miss me, but they'll be okay" she assured him.

"Good," he said. "Because I'd miss you more if I had to spend the night without the woman I love."

"I've decided that Christmas is my favorite time of year," Bailey announced to Serena the next morning.

"And when did you arrive at this conclusion?" she asked.

"Just now, when I woke up and you were here, and I had the incomparable pleasure of making love with my beautiful fiancée on December 25."

"I've always loved Christmas," she reminded

him. "But you've given me even more reasons to love it—and to look forward to all the Christmases we'll share together."

And as she snuggled in his arms and listened to the strong steady beat of his heart, she couldn't help but think of her sister and hope that wherever Mimi was—because with all of her heart and soul, Serena believed that her little sister was out there somewhere—she was also celebrating the holiday with someone she loved.

"I'm still not sure this is real," she said. "It seems like a dream."

"My dream come true," he told her.

"You really do want to marry me?"

"Why would you doubt it?"

"It just seems like everything happened so fast and—"

"Do *you* have doubts?" he interrupted to ask her.

"No," she immediately replied. "But I also never said that I'd never get married again."

"I did say that," he acknowledged. "Because I was sure it was true…and then I fell in love with you."

"So your proposal wasn't just an impulse?"

"The timing was a little impulsive," he admitted. "I probably should have waited to ask until I had a ring, but I promise as soon as stores open on December 26, I'll fix that oversight."

"I should probably say that I don't need a ring, but I want one. I want a visible symbol to show the world—or at least the rest of Rust Creek Falls—that I'm engaged to marry Bailey Stockton."

He shifted so that he was facing her, then lifted a hand to brush her hair away from her face and gently stroke her cheek. "I love you, Serena."

She smiled. "I love you, too."

They sealed their promises with another kiss, which might have led to more except that Bailey's cell phone buzzed on the bedside table. With obvious reluctance, he eased his lips from hers and picked up the offending instrument to read the text message on the screen.

"We're being summoned to the main house for breakfast and then gifts."

"Maybe I could borrow your truck and head back to my place to check on Marvin, Molly and Max," Serena suggested.

"If you're worried about them, we'll both go," he said.

"I'm not really worried," she admitted. "I just thought I should give you some time with your family."

"You're part of that family now, too," he reminded her.

So they got dressed and headed over to the main house, where everyone else was already gathered around the table overflowing with tasty offerings: platters of scrambled eggs, bacon and sausage, stacks of toast and bowls of fresh fruit.

"You're late," Jamie said when Bailey settled into a vacant chair beside him.

"I'd say I'm right on time," he countered, as Eva added a plate of sticky buns, fresh out of the oven, to the assortment of food already on the table.

"I want to know when it's nap time," Fallon confided. "We've been up for hours already with the triplets, and when we finish up here, we're heading over to my parents' place for Christmas Day—round three."

"I'm glad you were able to squeeze this into your schedule," Bella said sincerely.

"Are you kidding? This is the best part of the day," Fallon said to the woman who had been her friend long before she was her sister-in-law.

"It is special," Dana chimed in. "To be able to celebrate the holidays with all of you."

Of course, everyone was aware that the group was incomplete. Unless and until Liza was found, there would always be something missing. But for now, they focused on the joy of being together. And when everyone had eaten their fill, they retreated to the living room to disperse the presents that were piled under the tree.

"It's amazing, isn't it?" Annie said, nudging Bailey with her shoulder as the triplets attacked an enormous box that had all their names on it.

"What's amazing? The noise? The mess? The chaos?"

His sister-in-law laughed softly. "Well, all of that," she acknowledged. "Because it's all part and parcel of being a member of this family. But I was actually referring to the difference that a year can make."

"This time last year, you and Dan were newlyweds," Bailey noted.

"And you'd just returned to Rust Creek Falls,

a bitter and cynical Grooge, certain you weren't going to stay."

He couldn't deny that was true—or that, until only a few weeks ago, he'd remained mostly bitter and cynical and unconvinced that there was a future for him in this town. And then his brother and sister-in-law had conned him into donning Santa's hat and coat.

He'd totally been faking it that first day. He'd had no Christmas spirit of his own to share with the kids. Serena had helped him find not just that Christmas spirit again but closure on his past and hope for his future.

She'd changed everything for him.

"It's true," he agreed. "A lot can change in a year—or when you finally find the one person you're meant to spend the rest of your life with."

"You're welcome," Annie said.

"Yeah, maybe I do owe you for that," he acknowledged.

"And I know just how you can pay me back."

"How?" he asked, a little warily.

She smiled. "Be happy." Then she kissed his cheek and moved away to find her husband.

But Bailey knew that he already was.

As he looked around the room, he was grateful and humbled to be part of this crazy family whose connection and affection had not only endured but grown stronger over distance and time. Of course, their family had grown in size, too, with so many of his siblings pairing up and having babies. Or, in Dan and Annie's case, an almost-teenager.

He found Serena in the crowd, and felt his heart swell to fill his whole chest. She was sitting on the floor by the fire with Jared— or was that Henry?—on her lap. The nephew had a gingerbread cookie in his hand, which he would gnaw on for a while and then offer to Serena, and she would gamely take a nibble of the soggy treat before the little guy shoved it back in his own mouth.

She fit so perfectly here. With his family. With him.

Annie was right—a single year could make a world of difference. And he hoped that by next Christmas, Serena would be his wife rather than his fiancée. And maybe, not too long after that, they'd have a child of their own to contribute to the mayhem.

That thought gave him a moment's pause.

Henry—or was it Jared?—toddled over to his brother with two chunky toy trucks clutched in his fists, obviously hoping to entice him away from his cookie to play. His brother was happy to abandon his snack, but he kissed Serena's cheek before sliding from her lap, and she smiled as she watched the brothers move away.

Bailey found a napkin on a nearby table and offered it to her. She wrapped the remnants of the soggy cookie, then wiped the crumbs from her hand.

"You looked deep in thought over there," she commented, as he sat down beside her.

"I was just wondering how long it takes to plan a wedding," he said, sliding his arm around her shoulders.

"You can't be talking about our wedding."

"Why not?"

"Because we only just got engaged."

"Do you know why I asked you to marry me?"

"Because you love me and want to spend the rest of your life with me?"

"All of that," he agreed. "And because I want to start our life together as soon as possible."

"I want that, too."

"So let's set a date," he urged.

"Okay," she agreed. "June 25."

"That's six months away."

"I figure it will probably take that long to plan a wedding."

"Unless we get someone to do it for us," he noted. "Caroline Ruth did a great job with the Presents for Patriots event."

"She did," Serena agreed. "And now that you mention it, Sawmill Station would be the perfect venue for a wedding."

"Then I suggest we reach out to her as soon as possible to get started with the planning."

"What's your hurry?" she wondered.

"Well, I was thinking—" he tipped his head toward hers, his expression filled with cautious hope "—the sooner we get married, the sooner we can get started making a baby."

Her heart fluttered, yearned. "In that case," she said, her eyes growing misty, "the sooner the better."

It was an almost perfect day.

Of course, spending Christmas morning with

his siblings, it was natural that Bailey would think about the parents who were no longer with them. And while their absence tugged at his heart, he felt certain that Rob and Lauren Stockton were looking down on their children, happy to see them celebrating together.

Of course, they weren't all together. Not yet. But some of Serena's eternal optimism must have rubbed off on him, because he was starting to believe that the reunion of his siblings would soon be complete.

That thought had barely formed in his mind when the doorbell rang.

The sound didn't interrupt the festivities. Several of the adults exchanged curious glances, silently wondering who would be visiting on Christmas Day, then Luke went to discover the answer to that unspoken question.

A few minutes later, he returned with an unexpected but very welcome guest.

Bailey's heart hammered against his ribs as

he reached for Serena's hand and linked their fingers together.

"Liza."

It was Bella who first ventured to whisper the name, and the younger woman's familiar blue eyes immediately filled with tears.

Then, more loudly for the benefit of those who hadn't realized that someone new had joined the party, Bella announced, "Liza's home."

The rest of her siblings all rushed forward to embrace the long-lost sister who had finally returned.

Serena decided it was an appropriate time to extricate herself from the family gathering. Though she was thrilled for Bailey and all his brothers and sisters, their impromptu family reunion was a painful reminder that her family was still in pieces. Yes, she was starting to rebuild a relationship with her mother, but she still felt the loss of the father who'd walked out of her life fifteen years earlier and, even more deeply, the absence of the sister who had disappeared without a trace a year previous to that.

But Serena's efforts to slip away were thwarted by her fiancé.

"Where are you going?" Bailey asked her.

"Home," she said. "I've already been gone longer than I intended to be."

"Your SUV is in a ditch," he reminded her.

She held up the keys in her hand. "Eva's letting me borrow her vehicle."

"That's not necessary," he said. "I can take you."

"I know you can, but you've been waiting for this reunion a long time."

"And you're still waiting for yours," he realized.

"I am," she admitted. "But seeing you with your siblings, knowing you found your way back to one another after so many years apart, gives me renewed hope that I'll find Mimi again."

"You will," he said confidently.

"But in the meantime, my pets are waiting for me," she told him.

"So we'll go get Marvin, Molly and Max and bring them back here," he decided.

"Don't you think that will be a little...chaotic?"

"No, I think it will be *a lot* chaotic," he acknowledged. "But it's Christmas, and family should be together on Christmas."

"You got more than you bargained for, didn't you?" Serena remarked later, after she and Bailey had returned to the relative quiet of his cabin following dinner with his family—and hers. Because Amanda and Mark had been at her apartment when they went to get her pets, and Bailey had persuaded them to join the festivities at Sunshine Farm.

"It was every bit as chaotic as you promised," he confirmed. "And I wouldn't have changed a minute of it."

Marvin, Molly and Max might have agreed with his assessment, but they were already snuggled up together and asleep in the dog's bed, exhausted from so much attention and excitement.

"Grams didn't even protest being dragged away from her celebration on the beach to hear the news of our engagement," Serena noted.

"Although she did request that we plan a summer wedding."

"June 25 is summer," she pointed out, referencing the date she'd originally suggested.

"And it's a long time to wait to make you my wife," he grumbled.

"I know you're eager to get started on a family of our own, but a June wedding ensures we'll have lots of time to practice our baby-making technique."

"Are you suggesting that I need practice?" he asked, his tone indignant.

"Of course not," she soothed. "I'm only suggesting that I would very much enjoy practicing with you."

"Okay, then," he relented.

"In fact... I was kind of hoping we might practice tonight."

And that's just what they did—all night long.

Epilogue

"Did you hear the news?" glowing newlywed Vivienne Shuster Dalton asked her recently engaged friend and colleague Caroline Ruth.

"If you're referring to the news that Bailey Stockton proposed to Serena Langley on Christmas Eve, then yes, I did," Caroline confirmed.

"That's six engagements in the past six months."

"Love is definitely in the air in Rust Creek Falls," Caroline agreed.

"Fingers crossed—" Vivienne demonstrated

with her own "—we're going to be planning a lot of weddings in the upcoming year."

"But there are still a lot of single men and women in town," Caroline noted.

Vivienne clapped her hands together glee-fully. "Which promises even more business in years to come."

Although Caroline shared her business part-ner's optimism, she felt compelled to issue a word of caution. "Some of them might need a little nudge to set them on the right path."

"Oooh, you're right." Vivienne considered, then nodded. "That's a great idea."

Caroline wasn't sure how to respond to her colleague's unbridled enthusiasm. "What did I say? What's a great idea?"

"Adding matchmaking to our list of services."

"That wasn't my idea," she immediately pro-tested.

But now that it was out there, the possibili-ties were undeniably intriguing...

* * * * *

LET'S TALK
Romance

For exclusive extracts, competitions
and special offers, find us online:

f facebook.com/millsandboon

⊙ @millsandboonuk

🐦 @millsandboon

Or get in touch on 0844 844 1351*

For all the latest titles coming soon,
visit millsandboon.co.uk/nextmonth

*Calls cost 7p per minute plus your phone company's price per
minute access charge